George John Whyte-Melville

The Adventures of Jane Lee

Vol. 3

George John Whyte-Melville

The Adventures of Jane Lee
Vol. 3

ISBN/EAN: 9783337341183

Printed in Europe, USA, Canada, Australia, Japan

Cover: Foto ©Raphael Reischuk / pixelio.de

More available books at **www.hansebooks.com**

BLACK BUT COMELY

or,

THE ADVENTURES OF JANE LEE.

BY

G. J. WHYTE-MELVILLE.

IN THREE VOLUMES.

VOL. III.

London:

CHAPMAN AND HALL, 193, PICCADILLY.

1879.

DALZIEL BROTHERS,
CAMDEN PRESS, LONDON, N.W.

CONTENTS.

CHAPTER XLIV.

CHAPTER XLV.

CHAPTER XLVI.

CHAPTER XLVII.

CHAPTER XLVIII.

CHAPTER XLIX.

CHAPTER L.

CHAPTER LI.

CHAPTER LII.

CHAPTER LIII.

CHAPTER LIV.

CHAPTER LV.

CHAPTER LVI.

CHAPTER LVII.

CHAPTER LVIII.

CHAPTER LIX.

CHAPTER LX.

BLACK BUT COMELY;

OR,

THE ADVENTURES OF JANE LEE.

Book IV.

CHAPTER XL.

THE SECOND ACT.

THE audience have been judiciously packed, the
free list is represented in all parts of the house,
and rounds of applause greet the re-appearance
of Mr. Delaprè, dressed out in the height of
fashion as a stage dandy of uncertain period.
His wristbands are turned back over his coat-
cuffs, his boots are resplendent with varnish, his

frock-coat is buttoned, and he wears spurs, though ostensibly spending the evening with noblemen from every part of Europe in a Parisian resort furnished like a palace, which professes to be a high-class club devoted to high-class play.

Fruit, flowers, tall champagne - bottles, and pyramids of burnished plate, highly gilt, are piled upon a buffet at the back, while in front near the footlights is drawn a card-table, from which the players have lately risen, leaving great heaps of gold to mark the places where they sat.

Our friend the Hospodar seems to have been a heavy loser. He is accompanied by Count Randolph, and attended by Fritz, who carries a portfolio with an enormous lock and key. None of these have made the slightest alteration in their dress since we saw them last among the gipsies in the great forest. Their host's disguise, on the contrary, is so complete that they betray no suspicion of his identity, accepting

him, as it would seem, for a Prince of the Holy
Roman Empire, claiming no particular nation-
ality, and addressing him, for no obvious reason,
as "Excellency" at every second word.

Mr. Delaprè is playing his very best. It is
plain to see that he revels in his part. The high
and mighty manners, the overdone courtesies,
the bowing and bending and waving of arms,
are exceedingly to his taste, and he plumes himself on certain delicate by-play, in which he
suffers the habits of the vagrant to peep through
the polish of the gentleman, as when, after
quaffing a tall goblet of champagne, he wipes
his mouth on his coat-sleeve, and again, lighting
a cigar, holds the match in the hollow of his
two hands, like one who is accustomed to smoke
his pipe in the breezes of an open moor.

It is no sham cigar. Ladies in the farthest
row of the stalls can smell it distinctly, and the
audience are much gratified: they appreciate, no
doubt, a realism which, improving on Horace's

advice, thus appeals to a third sense for the truth of dramatic representation.

The Hospodar does not smoke. Perhaps his losses have affected his digestion : they seem to have been enormous, and have found their way into the pockets of the Prince. The loser clanks about the stage, nevertheless, with bombastic allusions to his serfs, his title-deeds, and his estates, quaffs champagne, turns his chair three times for luck, and sits down to play *ecarte* with the winner for what he calls " the doubtful hazard of the whole amount," or, in plain English, " double or quits."

Here the gipsy is in his element. Constant practice in fortune-telling has enabled him to do with the cards what he likes, and Mr. Delapré, shuffling the pack, lets his audience into the secret by performing two or three ingenious tricks. The Hospodar, in the meantime, summons Fritz with the portfolio, which seems to contain His Excellency's title-deeds, and prepares to join battle with all the resources at his command.

It is a thousand pities that our business and, for that matter, our pleasures, cannot be disposed of as expeditiously in real life as on the stage. An actor, with a slap on its page, reads a letter at one sidelong glance, and dashes off a cheque for a thousand in a quarter the time it takes you or me to write one for a hundred. He is no more dilatory at his toilet or his meals. Three turns of his cloak, and one pull at his hat, serve for complete disguise. He can drink to intoxication in a few seconds, and his dinner is finished almost as soon as he has sat down. It is no wonder, then, that in two of the quickest games ever played at cards, the Hospodar should have lost all his ready money and available resources; so that, in a hollow voice, betraying uncontrollable agitation, he challenges his antagonist to a third, unlocking the portfolio handed him by Fritz, and placing on the table, as his stakes, a small document tied up in red tape, purporting to be the title-deeds of his Podolian estates.

Count Randolph and Fritz are looking on. The company, leaving their own games unfinished, have gathered round. Mr. Delapré, cutting the pack, performs, deftly enough, yet so distinctly that it is patent to his audience, the old trick of palming the king, and marks him with a diabolical scowl, that changes through a sneer to a smile, as he meets his adversary's eye.

The Hospodar shades his brow with his hand. When he withdraws it, his face is deadly pale. He trembles so that he can hardly deal the cards, and presently, uttering an exclamation of despair, rises, advances to the footlights, and proclaims to prompter, fiddlers, and occupiers of the stalls, that he is a ruined man!

It seems, however, that the amusements are to conclude with a ball, given by the club; for at this juncture the card-tables are cleared away, the back of the stage discloses a brilliant chandelier, and crowded dancing-room; couples advance to the front, officers in red, diplomatists in blue, ladies rouged, jewelled, and in the shortest petticoats. Lufra, now Her Excellency, the admired of all, whirls away for a waltz in Count Randolph's arms. The Hospodar stands immovable, staring into vacancy; Mr. Delaprè, posing for Mephistopheles, contemplates his victim; the drop-scene falls, and Beltenebrosa, taking courage to steal a look round, finds Lord St. Moritz has vanished, and his place is occupied by a young man she never saw before.

Now, during the conclusion of the foregoing act, there had been as much by-play on one side of the footlights as on the other. Lord St. Moritz was resolved to have a word with Beltenebrosa when she left the theatre, but did not see his way to an interview so long as he was in charge of Mrs. Stripwell, whom he could not leave unattended in such a place as this. Catching sight of "poor Algy" in the back of a private box, and stimulated perhaps by the genius of the locality, a plan of escape occurred to him, which he lost no time in carrying out.

The evening was mild, the house crowded; Mrs. Stripwell fanned herself without cessation, for, although in winter, the temperature was unpleasantly high.

"You feel it, I see," he whispered in his companion's pretty little ear, which had turned a deeper pink than usual. "Don't it make you quite faint?"

"Faint!" she repeated in the same tone, with some scorn; "not a bit. Why should it? What makes you ask?"

"Simply because I feel so myself, Mrs. Stripwell: don't consider me a brute if I desert you for ten minutes to get a breath of fresh air. Think what a false position I should be in if I fainted dead away anywhere but at your feet!"

"There wouldn't be much room," she answered, laughing. "And I won't have you on my knee. Yes, you'd better go, and come back when you feel better."

So he snatched up his hat and overcoat, to sidle out with many apologies over the feet and dresses of some half-score acquaintances.

Once clear, he lost no time in finding the box occupied by "poor Algy," and tapping at the door, which was opened by that Guardsman himself, called him into the passage.

"Algy," said he, "you can do me a great favour, and I think it will be no trouble to you: taking care of the ladies is all in your line."

"What is it?" asked Algy, not very cordially disposed towards his visitor, but mollified—as who would not be at twenty?—by the inference his compliment conveyed.

"Well, I'm obliged to leave the theatre, you see, and Mrs. Stripwell has no one to look after her. Would you mind taking my place, and getting her carriage, and all that? Will it bore you?"

Bore him! Did it bore William of Deloraine to look on daylight once more when he had lingered "long months three in dungeon dark" of the feudal enemy he yearned to see restored to life that he might have the pleasure of killing him on his own account? Does it bore the camels of the desert, the oxen of the Transvaal, to see and smell the water-pool for which their very hearts are athirst? Does it bore the Swiss to revisit his mountains, the miser to reclaim his gold, the bee to revel in the petals of the rose? Algy seemed so much bored with his Lordship's request, he could hardly gasp out a delighted assent.

"The stall is number eleven," said the latter, buttoning up his coat: "this side of the house; you will have no difficulty in finding it. Tell her I'm very much afraid I shall not be able to come back."

I wonder what he *did* tell her when he sank into the seat by her side with a feeling of actual physical relief, after the tortures of pique, vexation, and jealousy undergone in the private box from which he had been watching the graceful head and white shoulders that could never be his own—that, his better reason often told him, wouldn't if they could. What folly, what madness it all was! And yet to this day he can look back on the short, sweet, sinful dream, as his one glimpse into fairyland. Yes, when our eyes are touched with the enchanted herb, this bewildering region looks like the true Paradise; but few of us have Thomas the Rhymer's luck to escape before that fatal term arrives which renders us amenable to the tax from hell.

All he *did* say, depend upon it, was not a quarter of what was in his head, a tithe of what was in his heart. She would have liked him better, perhaps, had he been more voluble and less sincere.

He was young, and could therefore plead more excuse for his folly than Lord St. Moritz

The one drowned heart, brain, and senses in a deep full draught of intoxication; the other, like an habitual dram-drinker, kept up his excitement with frequent sips, always willing to partake, wherever offered, of the stimulating glass.

It has been observed by more than one author that the devil is never so busy with a man as while he is waiting for a woman.

It must have been a pertinacious little imp who was whispering in his Lordship's ear, as he turned up the collar of his coat and lit a cigar to hang about the deserted street at the door of the play-house. He felt he had made sure of Beltenebrosa by his speedy exit. Whether she left early or late, he could not miss her now, and the very fact of her being in London argued a loneliness that must prove favourable to his advances. How noble she looked while she turned her profile to examine the house! Mourning only added to the brilliancy of her eyes and smile. She was pale, indeed, but no paler than usual; perhaps a trifle fuller in figure than when he saw her last at Combe-Wester, and, if possible, more beautiful. She had not been pining for *him*, that seemed clear enough, and he liked her all the better. Where would he ever see such a woman again? What was Lady Goneril—what were a hundred Mrs. Stripwells compared to this paragon? Why not marry her now she was free, and become a respectable member of society once more?

If the little imp had only whispered, "Perhaps she wouldn't marry *you*," his Lordship might have thought of the matter seriously; but it did nothing of the kind: on the contrary, it reminded him of his many conquests, of his general popularity, of his experiences with the unfortunate lady now in her grave, whom he had once led to the altar; and again came over him the insuperable aversion to domestic restraint that had become ingrained in his very being.

"There is no occasion for the sacrifice," he said to himself, wondering how long this third act would last, and what excuse he should make to Madame Paravant, *née* Beltenebrosa, for intruding himself so far as to ask for a lift in her carriage home. Of course she had a carriage; if a hired brougham, so much the better: its driver would be devoid of curiosity on any subject unconnected with beer. Of interruption from Mrs. Stripwell he had no fear. That lady could keep a dozen admirers on hand with perfect equanimity, but the one who was present always had the call, and he felt persuaded she would have eyes and ears only for the blissful Algy, if she came out of the house on his arm, and permitted him to wind a provoking little cloud of woollen work she affected round her dainty chin.

"How he doats on her, poor boy!" thought Lord St. Moritz, turning in his walk at the nearest lamp-post, with a cynical smile. "He loves the very ground she treads, and thinks she can do no wrong. What a fool he is! and, by Jove, what a fool I am too! I'll be hanged if it isn't beginning to rain!"

CHAPTER XLI.

It seems a pity to lose the last act, culminating in a catastrophe by no means original, but sufficiently far-fetched to delight a public that, naturally enough, require on the stage improbabilities more striking than it meets with at home.

Beltenebrosa, thoroughly interested in the action of the piece, suffers not a word nor look of the principal performer to escape her, following Mr. Delaprè with her eyes in such earnest attention as would be exceedingly flattering to that gentleman were he not so absorbed in his own part that he can think of nothing else. His place, too, is at the back of the scene, which now represents a terrace opening from the ball-room, studded with huge stone vases full of flowers, overlooking gardens like those of Versailles— silvered with sparkling fountains, gemmed in coloured lamps, and bordered by a dim, well wooded landscape, that stretches to the horizon under a pale glimmer of dawn. In front, while striding to and fro as contemplating some des-perate measure, the Hospodar imparts to that eligible confidant, Hussar Fritz, his irremediable ruin, and the fatal resolution it compels him to adopt.

"The bark," says he, launching on the strain of metaphor in which a man ordinarily addresses his valet, "reft of its helm, drives hopeless to the rock! Stripped of her plumes, the eagle falls to earth!"

Fritz stares—as well he may—while Mr. Delaprè, cloaked to the chin, and not the least concealed by the stone vases behind which he prowls, mutters "Hist!" very loud and with

such emphasis as calls attention to a coming
declaration from the Hospodar, that he means to
blow his own brains out before sunrise. Fritz,
much affected, but preserving the comic side of
his character, endeavours to dissuade his master
from so irrevocable a step, reminding him of
Lufra, when the Hospodar embarks in a high-
flown and tedious harangue, enlarging on the
many estimable qualities of that young person,
and his regret, which seems in no way to affect
his determination, that they must soon be parted
for ever; concluding that he will "retire to yonder chamber for an hour, to pen the last directions and farewell. This friendly weapon, loaded
to my hand, acquittance shall afford with full
release. And harkye! even as to-morrow's
sun comes up, my Fritz, the Hospodar goes
down!"

So this doomed nobleman "retires up," and
the Prince comes forward from behind his flower-
vases to dash a tear-drop from his eye, and smite

his breast hard with clenched fist, as denoting intentions of immediate action, to be explained · in a soliloquy, that is happily interrupted by the appearance of Lufra in her ball-dress, kissing her fingers to a partner she has left at the wings, obviously on her way to husband, cloak-room, carriage, and bed.

Startled by the presence of His Excellency, whom she does not in the least recognize for her gipsy lover, she nevertheless gives him her hand with touching confidence. Mr. Delapré having the stage to himself, plays up to the situation with unbounded satisfaction. Pique, scorn, jealousy, and, to use the powerful language of the dramatist,

> "The ashes of an unextinguished fire,
> That burned so fiercely once in this fond heart,
> Whose tablets bear the brand of Lufra's name
> Scored to the quick in characters of flame!"

—all this has to be represented, besides a sentiment of generosity that struggles hard with less

worthy considerations, and gains the ascendancy
at last.

"Charles Kean could have done it," thinks
Mr. Delaprè, "and perhaps Macready; nobody
else that ever walked the boards, I firmly believe,
but your humble servant!"

His Excellency, assuming the port of Mario as
Don Giovanni in the supper scene, a delineation
of the polished *roué* that can never be surpassed,
congratulates the lady on her looks, her dress,
her dancing, and her good spirits. She is happy
no doubt, as she *deserves* to be, with her husband;
and he! what an enviable lot seems his! How
true the proverb that love makes amends to
those who have bad luck at cards! Bad luck!
She suspected, nay, she feared it. His Excellency
must not detain her; she ought to be at her
husband's side in his distress. He loves her, do
you see? and nobody else can console him!

His Excellency would not detain her on any
consideration, but he does not let go of her hand,

catechizing her with a persistency for which he deserved to have his ears boxed. Does she love the Hospodar honestly, from the bottom of her heart? Has she no thoughts but for him? Does she never spare one single sigh for another?

Lufra covers her face with her hands—the best actress cannot blush through a quarter of an inch of paint—and confesses by her disorder that it is possible there might be a somebody else, only the Hospodar is so kind, so indulgent, so fond of her. No, she would be miserable away from him. She must go to him now! Gipsy John is touched, believing himself not wholly forgotten.

And if the Hospodar were in trouble, argues His Excellency, pursuing the unwelcome subject, if he were in difficulties, if he were *r-r-ruined!* and by his own folly, what then? Would she not leave him to his fate, and take refuge with that other for whom she yet cherishes some kindly remembrance in her heart? How can he ask?

His Excellency might find more worthy themes for jesting than a woman's holiest feelings, or is this done to try her? Were the Hospodar ruined, nay, were he even disgraced, she would fly to him the faster, bringing help if she could, love, sympathy, and comfort, if help were beyond her power.

A husband never needed more the presence of his wife, continues His Excellency, observing that he scorns to jest or trifle; his heart is too heavy; and only in deep and desperate play can it find distraction from undying regret. At such a pastime fortune favoured him to-night. He has won from the Hospodar everything that noble-man possessed in the world, except (with a satanic grin) his wife. If she believes him not, he can furnish proof. There!—he flings at her feet the document before mentioned, tied up in its red tape. Here are the title-deeds conveying posses-sion of castles, forests, serfs—in short, a whole principality within the frontiers of Podolia. Hold!

for she pounces at it like a kitten at its ball.
That little packet is worth a king's ransom, shall
it not purchase a woman's smile? Ah! will she
not think kindly of one who can thus sacrifice the
revenues of a kingdom for her sake?

Here Mr. Delaprè, taking another leaf out of
Mario's book, as Faust in the garden, does some
strenuous love-making—so impassioned, indeed,
that Mrs. Stripwell in the stalls feels less displeasure at the signs Lufra begins to show of
relenting than surprise she should have held out
so long! If Algy could only act like this, or any
of them, what a much pleasanter world we should
have! How delightful to be assailed in blank
verse, with long-resounding periods and dramatic
gestures to correspond! Why, oh, why could
her own admirers never soar beyond " tremen-
dously fetching " and " awfully nice " ?

There are some things, not many, that a man
does better in sport than in earnest. The less
respect he entertains for his listeners, the better

he succeeds when making speeches or making love. In such rhetorical flights a familiarity, born of constant practice, alone ensures success. Maiden efforts are usually clumsy productions enough, and the House of Commons, I have been given to understand, is exceedingly tolerant of awkwardness in a first essay; but the more practical sex are by no means so indulgent in taking the will for the deed; and a suitor is likely enough to find himself non-suited who boggles, stammers, and cannot get out what he means.

Mr. Delaprè, either on or off the stage, is a glib wooer enough, and seems to advance rapidly in the good graces of Lufra, perhaps reminding her of some one who has made love to her before; but time and the prompter wait for no man : a sudden brightening of the whole stage with a tinge of crimson thrown from the sides, that, again to quote the dramatist,

"Flushes with rosy light the eastern sky,"

—serves to warn His Excellency that the sun is rising, and no time must be lost if the Hospodar is to be prevented "going down" by his own hand.

Lufra is in possession of the title-deeds. She has kissed and placed them in her bosom with many professions of gratitude in dumb show. Taking her by the tips of her fingers, as if to lead her out in a minuet, the Prince conducts her to the back of the stage, both walking, for no obvious reason, with extreme caution, on their toes.

Count Randolph, still in his frock-coat and Hessians, appears for a moment at the side-scenes, expressing by his gestures extreme solicitude for Her Excellency, whom he seems to have been watching since she left the ball-room. Making signs of caution not to be noticed by the Prince, Lufra points to her bosom, as if to assure the Count she has got something safe in that enviable lurking-place; and he retires, also on tiptoe.

apparently well satisfied. The orchestra now plays a few bars in a low key, suggestive of mystery, and indeed apprehension, from "The Lohengrin," while the whole stage becomes obscured, which would be surprising at sunrise did one not remember that the darkest hour of night comes immediately before day! As the music dies out in low, faint, trembling chords, double doors open at the back of the stage, to discover, in a room furnished for a bed-chamber, the Hospodar leaning pensively against a window-frame, to watch the widening dawn. Fritz is at hand with a case of duelling pistols, standing in an attitude of respectful and soldierlike attention, prepared to obey orders without demur.

The Hospodar, murmuring farewell to Podolia, and maundering about "his hordes of horsemen" left without a chief, takes one of the weapons from its case, to load it with the utmost nicety, glancing the while at that ever-brightening horizon on which the crimson has now turned

to gold. As the rim of an exceedingly red sun
peeps above the sky-line, he cocks his pistol, and
presses it to his forehead. One moment, and
Podolia would lose her lord! but his arm is
caught and held down by Lufra, who hangs
about his neck, assuring him, with tears and
sobs and wild caresses, that, thanks to their
preserver — to wit, His Excellency — they are
saved !

The Prince looks sternly on, and Count
Randolph, who has followed the others, tries to
stand aside in an easy attitude, feeling, no doubt,
that his presence here is uncalled for and superfluous.

Charged to explain, Lufra, followed by the
whole party, advances to the footlights, and with
a redundancy of action that displays her well-
turned bust and powdered arms to great advantage, draws from her bosom the important title-
deeds, to present them in conjugal affection to
her husband. With these flies out an envelope

that falls at the Hospodar's feet, who, naturally enough, picks it up, and is about to return it politely, when his attention is arrested by the start and half-suppressed shriek of the owner, who flings her hands above her head in a gesture of despair. Count Randolph, too, seems disturbed, advancing with the established half-stride, full stop, and regulation glare.

The Hospodar, pistol in hand, looks from one to the other, tears open the paper, and finds what he is pleased to term " the blasting sight " of the Count's photograph, with certain impassioned lines that leave no doubt of his wife's infidelity. He raises his arm and covers his enemy with deadly aim; Lufra throws herself at his feet in wild despair; His Excellency, emerging from his cloak, stands revealed as Gipsy John, contemplating the group with scowls of fiendish scorn, and the curtain falls; while Mrs. Stripwell, collecting her wraps, hastens into the passage, not waiting to see Mr. Delaprè lead Miss

Mountcharles across a narrow strip of stage at
the footlights, with many sidelong bows and
obeisances to acknowledge the ovation in which
the audience bid them good night.

"What do you think of it?" she asks Algy,
on whose arm she leans, rather heavily, he flatters
himself.

Algy never enjoyed a play so much : he would
like to bring her here every night. Why can't
he say so, instead of blundering out irrelevant
remarks concerning Miss Mountcharles, her
rouge, her figure, and personal advantages, on
or off the stage?

Beltenebrosa has nobody to take care of *her*.
How different from last season, she thinks rather
bitterly, and not without a twinge of regret for
the dead husband who had enough generosity
to be proud of the admiration accorded to his
wife.

She missed him more than usual to-night,
and could not help thinking how conveniently

those sturdy shoulders of his would have forced
a passage for her through the crowd streaming
to the door.   She fell back to let them pass, and
was one of the last to leave the theatre.   When
she came out it was raining hard, and not a cab
to be seen.

CHAPTER XLII.

OUT OF QUOD.

Lord St. Moritz stood at her elbow. " Good
heavens, Signora ! " he exclaimed, using the old
familar expression, " what an unexpected meeting ! How delightful to see you once more ! but
you can't stand talking here, you'll be wet to the
skin. Where is your carriage ? Take my arm,
and let me get you a cab."

Mechanically she obeyed. There were some
rough people about, and a drunken woman was
screaming horrible oaths. Lord St. Moritz
seemed no unwelcome escort, and—yes, after
her long seclusion, it was refreshing to meet an
admirer again.

At the first lamp-post they hailed a passing cab, the driver of which, an old man, was wrapped in coat and comforter to the eyes. Before she had time to think what she was doing, Lord St. Moritz asked her address, handed her in, gave the cabman directions, took his place by her side, and shut the door with a bang. The next moment they were jolting along a badly-lighted, badly-paved street, and he was shaking hands with her, quite unnecessarily, a second time.

I imagine no vehicle in the world is so ill adapted for confidential disclosures, or even general conversation, as a four-wheeled cab. It is confined, uncomfortable, and noisy. If the windows are down, mud splashes in from every puddle; if you pull them up, they jingle so that you cannot hear yourself speak. The cushions are too often dirty and damp, the seats sloping and narrow; the whole interior redolent of stale tobacco-smoke, mould, and manure. Perhaps, all these disagreeables combined causing Beltenebrosa to desire the conclusion of her drive, led her to notice the streets through which they passed, and to suspect they were taking a round-about way home.

Like her kinsfolk, she was gifted with an instinctive knowledge of locality, and having seen a place once, would always recognize it again by day or night. She was quite sure she had passed none of these lanes and byways on her way to the Nonsuch Theatre from South Kensington. Some idea of the insult he was trying to put on her roused her temper to the utmost. She desired, in a loud and angry tone, to be set down at once. The words had hardly passed her lips when the cab came to a sudden stop; a heavy figure descended hurriedly from the box; the door swung open; a powerful hand was laid on Lord St. Moritz's collar, and a hoarse voice exclaimed in the familiar accents of Fighting Jack, barely six weeks out of prison,

"Blowed if I worn't sure of it! Blessed if

it ain't my lass!—my lass that I never thought
to set eyes on to again. Don't you be skeered,
my pretty. This here swell must be a better
man than I take him for if he offers to lay a
hand on ye while your old father can stand up
to see fair."

Thus speaking, he pulled Lord St. Moritz out
of the vehicle by main force, with a jerk that
sent him reeling some paces along the footway.
His Lordship's blood was up, and without a
moment's reflection he advanced on the cabman
with his fists clenched, in an attitude that showed
he was not unpractised in the art of self-defence.
The old professional laughed with a grim satisfaction almost amounting to good-humour. After
his long imprisonment it was *delicious*—nothing
else—to open his shoulders and feel the play of
his salient muscles once again. He stopped the
other's blows coolly, and only sparred at first as
if for the mere pleasure of the thing, till his fighting instinct grew too strong, and, drawing him-

self together, he sent in one of his terrible left-handers—foot, body, arm, and shoulder lending their whole force to a blow before which Lord St. Moritz went down as if he had been shot.

"The cove worn't much of a glutton," said the old gipsy, relating the circumstances subsequently, with a calm reflective smile. "A' knowed when he'd got enough. But there! to see him come in on purpose, like, with his guard anywheres and his mouth open!—flesh and blood couldn't abide the temptation, and I *let him have it!*"

At the moment, however, it seemed just possible his Lordship, who lay perfectly senseless, might never get up again, and a policeman's heavy tread echoing through the neighbouring street, Fighting Jack sprang hastily to the box, put his horse into the best apology for a gallop the poor old broken-down jade could afford, and only stopped for further directions when he had come a good mile from the scene of combat.

That unscrupulous gentleman, whom the passing policeman, with a strong notion that he was in liquor, now occupied himself in restoring to consciousness, had omitted to give the cabman Mrs. Paravant's proper address. It was late at night, or rather early in the morning, when Fighting Jack set his daughter down at her own door, refusing, with more delicacy of feeling than might have been expected, a hospitable entreaty that he would come upstairs to refresh himself after his late encounter.

"Not at present, I thank ye, my lass," said Jack, with affectionate politeness; "and I'll not take no fare, neither, not from *you*, my pretty! Dry? In course I'm dry—I'm allus dry. That's wot's the matter o' me. But I knows the rights —wot I calls the bearings—of things, as well as here and there one. Father or no father, daughter or no daughter, I ain't fit company for a lady's drawing-room, not till I've a-been home and cleaned myself, and seen to the horse, and taken

my forty winks, maybe, and a whiff of a pipe.
That's neither here nor there, but to-morrow's a
new day."

Looking at her progenitor as he went his
way, Beltenebrosa could not but observe how
the weighty arm of the law had bent his powerful
frame, and how a few months of penal servitude
had added years to his age.

His shaggy brows, once black as jet, were now
grizzled, and the dark eyes that used to flash so
brightly beneath them had become blear and
dim. He stooped, too, and though his frame was
large and muscular still, he seemed no longer a
tower of strength, but rather a fine old ruin
mouldering to decay. Like many another athlete,
Jack had taken liberties with his constitution,
and feeling little inconvenience from their effects
had indulged in ardent spirits with the freedom
that too surely entails its own punishment. Cold,
fever, privation, excessive watching, unreasonably
hard work—these are inimical to longevity, but

not one of them, nor all put together, can kill a man so surely as gin! It cuts his throat as effectually as a knife, only not from the outside. When Beltenebrosa last saw him on Swansdown Racecourse more than a year ago, Fighting Jack, to use his own expression, was " in the hands of the Philistines."

These did not get possession of his person without having to pay pretty dear for their prize. Up or down, rough-and-tumble, boxing, wrestling, or contending with his fellow-man in any other way, the old gipsy was a thorough proficient, for attack or defence. One policeman got his nose broke, another gave his evidence before the magistrates with a fearful pair of black eyes, and a third, brought into court in an arm-chair, swore with much circumstantial detail in which there was not a particle of truth, that the prisoner had bitten his finger and stamped on him when he was down.

" I 'd scorn to do it! " said Jack in unaffected

indignation. "No, your Worships, I've taken and given punishment as free as most, but I never hit a man a foul blow in my life, and I never will."

As this was the only defence he chose to offer, he found himself committed for trial on more than one serious charge; and although his people made up a good purse of money to retain a counsel who knew every outlet of the law, and witnesses prepared to perjure themselves to any extent, it was no use. A sufficiently lenient judge did but his duty when he sentenced Fighting Jack to a long spell of imprisonment with hard labour in the county gaol.

For this child of the wilderness such confinement was double the punishment it would have been for the inhabitant of a town. The tough old vagrant pined like a love-sick girl for the song of the birds, the flutter of leaves, the glint of the morning sun on a running stream. Till he was deprived of them, he never knew

that these were necessary to his existence as the
food he ate, the air he breathed. Had his seclusion in that bare clean whitewashed cell lasted
but a few weeks longer, he believed it would
have killed him; and old Jack, forced to spend
in meditation the leisure he used to beguile with
beer and tobacco, wondered what would have
become of him then. Was the parson in down-
right earnest when he told those surprising
yarns concerning the two future states? or only
earning his day's pay, and jawing against time—
"sparring for wind" the old boxer called it—
because it seemed his duty to have something
to say? Altogether, he was disposed to believe
that his dissolution would, by some inexplicable
process of transmutation, identify him with the
world of nature and the elements he loved, to be
about in the morning mists that rolled along the
moor, the evening breeze that stirred the leafy
brake, hovering in company with his beautiful
Shuri, the wife he had not forgotten in twenty

years, over the haunts they knew so well and loved so dearly long long ago.

He was no atheist : few men are. He entertained some vague notions of a mighty governing Power, a Supreme Being to whom he felt grateful for health, strength, warmth, and sunshine, but whom he believed profoundly indifferent to the doings of mankind, or if concerning Himself on occasion with so inferior an order, according to gipsies a liberty of action not enjoyed by the rest of the human race.

Jack drew an extremely wide margin for his system of ethics, but would by no means pass his own line of demarcation between right and wrong. Perhaps when he sold his famous fight in the pride of his pugilistic fame, he felt more like doing evil than on any other occasion. He told himself many a time, and did not forget to repeat the reflection in prison, that " things had never gone right with him since, all round ! "

When he left the gaol, with empty pockets

and an enfeebled frame—for in spite of whole-
some diet and enforced temperance, the fretting
had worn him down—he scarcely knew where
to turn for a livelihood. Society is not disposed
to employ a gipsy at best, but on a gipsy fresh
out of prison the most liberal will inevitably turn
a cold shoulder. The *status ante* is always a
difficult position to resume; for none more so
than the culprit who has been condemned by
the laws of society, though he may have worked
out his sentence in full. We sin against God,
and find pardon without punishment over and
over again; we sin against man, are beaten with
many stripes, and seem never to be freely forgiven after all.

Though the old gipsy could turn his hand to
most things, he had no implements for the pro-
secution of his former occupations, and a certain
dogged sense of honesty, somewhat rare in his
race, forbade the obvious resource of stealing to
obtain daily bread. A man cannot make a basket

without withies, nor mend a kettle without tools; and but for the timely help of a Prisoners' Aid Society, Fighting Jack must have starved. He received the welcome gratuity with an astonishment that drowned every other sentiment, even gratitude.

"Then there *is* chaps in the world," said he, "and high chaps, too, as will pick a man up when he's down! Well, I *am*—a——"

He might have expressed himself in less reprehensible language; but from that day forth, the gipsy thought better of his neighbour, especially his neighbour in purple and fine linen, who fared sumptuously every day.

His self-respect made the old man averse to seeking out his tribe, who were, besides, at the other end of the kingdom, and applying to them for the assistance that, according to their patriarchal notions, he could claim as a right. He had always been comparatively well-to-do amongst these followers, who called him their Patron, and it seemed a humiliation to ask where he was accustomed to give. Yet he longed wearily to be with them again: yearned for the ragged tents, smouldering fires, and steaming kettles, no less cruelly than did Kingsley's dying chief for the wild and spacious plains of his Tartar home, while he moaned his last wish :

"I would I were back in Cauca-land,
    To hear my herdsmen's horn,
And to watch the waggons and brown brood
        mares,
    And the tents where I was born."

After knocking about the mews and stable-yards of London, Fighting Jack, whose knowledge of horseflesh was not to be despised, succeeded at last in obtaining employment as the driver of a four-wheeled cab, and found the situation, which involved much consumption of spirits in the open air, tolerably to his taste.

He was "down on his luck," though, the wet night Lord St. Moritz hailed him, and had not taken five shillings since breakfast. Wrapped in

his shabby old box-coat, he was driving doggedly
on, concerning himself in no way with the destination of his fare, lost in a train of thought that
carried him with his Shuri far into the past, when
in a moment, through the roll and jingle of his
vehicle, her unforgotten voice, raised in accents
of alarm and anger, thrilled to his very heart.
In one second he woke from his dream, the next
he recognized his daughter, and having lost little
of his promptitude for action, a third scarcely
elapsed ere he had leapt down to her rescue, and
gone in with fatal effect at the offending nobleman, who ought to have known better than to
be there at all.

CHAPTER XLIII.

POOR RELATIONS.

"No! my dear; but thank ye kindly, just the same; there ain't no call for the like of me to bide along of the like of ye. Not that I could bear to part with ye—never think it! But there! I don't seem to get my health, not sleeping night after night under the same roof, and my meals doesn't do me no good, not if I'm fed regular like a swine! Now, I shouldn't wonder if you had silver forks every day!"

Beltenebrosa could not honestly deny it, and felt perhaps less disappointed than she chose to appear at the disinclination to share his daughter's home which her vagabond parent evinced.

Looking at him by daylight, though he had
" cleaned himself " as he threatened, there
certainly seemed a want of finish in his appearance that was less striking outside a cab than
inside a drawing-room. His clothes were shabby,
indeed squalid, but that could be rectified ; soap
and water, too, applied more freely, would have
done much for the improvement of face and
hands. Such details were of little importance ;
the real curse that had come upon the man was
obvious at a glance : his whole person wore the
sodden look of one whose chief nutriment is
gin. It needed no experience in such matters to
convince her that the old gipsy had become a
confirmed drunkard, and it was to her credit
that Beltenebrosa should have felt a kindly and
filial impulse to cure him if she could.

When he called to see her the morning after
their adventure, she frankly invited him to come
and live with her, moved partly by feelings of
gratitude and affection, partly by a sense of lone-

liness forcibly brought home to her in the events of the previous night. She could provide for him, she said, she had enough for two. Living under her roof he would be sheltered from exposure to the elements, and—and—would not require quantities of alcohol to withstand their effects.

Perhaps he saw her drift, for there is no vice so sensitive to discovery or so averse to counsel as habitual drunkenness; perhaps a knowledge of the world he had not quite forgotten warned him such companionship *must* prove distasteful to both, or, more probably still, he felt under *surveillance* in the presence of this superior being, though she *was* his daughter, and longed, especially since his imprisonment, for unrestricted liberty of speech and action. So they made an agreement, like most compromises, to the satisfaction of neither, that Jack should take lodgings in the vicinity, which he immediately did at the nearest public house, should have access to the society of his daughter at stated hours, and that, although no consideration would induce him to pollute with tobacco such splendid apartments, yet, as of course there was usually " wine on the table," he could sit with her in the afternoons while she cleaned up, did her bit of needlework or what not, to partake of a cheerful glass.

Then the gipsy, receiving a trifle of wages due, discharged himself from his employer, and disappeared for eight and forty hours, where or how Beltenebrosa forbore to inquire, not caring to learn that he spent the whole interval between the floor and table of a tap-room, dead drunk. Who has not pitied Sindbad the Sailor for his Old Man of the Sea? For many days Beltene- brosa bore her *incubus* with exemplary patience and resignation. She let him sit by her side hour after hour through the short winter after- noons, so soon dark even in South Kensington, and the long candlelight evenings that dragged so wearily till he went away to what he called his " bit of supper," listening to his maunderings over the wine he insisted on sipping in honour of the position, though he would have much preferred gin. She even nursed him through a sharp fit of "the horrors," tending him with courage and forbearance, notwithstanding that her nerves were sadly shaken by the old gipsy's powers of imagination and description when he fancied himself in another world. She hoped this would have cured him ; but, no : though he trembled and cried like a child, with humble promises of amendment in his utter prostration, no sooner did strength return than he resumed his former habits, and took to drinking worse than ever.

Nor was this all. In some of the various haunts he frequented he came across his kinsman Jericho : no longer the Jericho of former days— blithe, free-hearted, and, except in the matter of game and poultry, comparatively honest ; but Jericho a confirmed knave and ruffian, who had

graduated through the sciences of chain-drop-
ping, shoplifting, and picking pockets; into an
accomplished criminal, ready for any scheme
of plunder however iniquitous, and living in
ease, almost affluence, on the proceeds of his
villany.

Old Jack's arrest had indeed served to break
up the gang : deprived of their leader, they were
like sheep without a bell-wether for courage, like
pirates without a captain for ferocity. The community became totally disorganized, and it was
a mercy—to use Jericho's pious expression—that
they did not turn to and rob one another! Perhaps they only escaped this last degradation
because there was so little to take. Tent after
tent, family after family, seceded from the en-
campment, drifting on their several courses to
all parts of the kingdom. Some wandered into
Yorkshire, some crossed the border to Kirk-
Getholm in Scotland; a few, amongst them
Jericho, cast up at Norwood, Shepherd's Bush,

and other haunts near London. Nance married
a tinker. This they felt a great blow and deep
disgrace, for the favoured suitor could boast only
the slightest cross of gipsy blood in his veins.
He had certain merits, no doubt, being a returned
convict and expert thief; but it was a deplor-
able alliance, in Jericho's opinion, and but for
the Patron's absence would never have taken
place.

"Wot, they missed the old man, did 'em?"
said Jack, when his former follower detailed these
particulars of a lost empire. "Ah! them was
good times for us all, when I used to hang out
in the old caravan, and never a Romany of our
own lot knew wot it was to want a drain, come
when he would, morning, noon, or night. But
it's not such a bad berth, Jerry, as I've chanced
to run against here, though I *do* miss the roll of
the old wheels; and if it wasn't for drink, a man
would go mad, to open his eyes on the same out-
look every morning of his life!"

Then Jack explained how and where he had again chanced on his daughter, launching into so flowery a description of her wealth, and the luxury in which she lived, as roused all the cupidity of Jericho's nature, and determined him to resume the working of a fertile field that had lain fallow much too long.

After Paravant's fatal accident, he would doubtless have followed up the widow, for Jericho allowed no sentimental considerations to interfere with that unscrupulous annexation of property which he considered the real business of life, but for one serious difficulty,—a case of passing base coin, in the county of Middlesex, which necessitated seclusion for an allotted period, and an avoidance for some time to come of the district in which he had made himself too conspicuous.

London also is a very large place, where people miss each other quite as unaccountably as they meet, and Jericho was deeply concerned to think that Jane Lee, relict of the rich Mr.

Paravant, had slipped through his fingers once for all, so the minute intelligence received from his old Patron was welcome as unexpected.

The two men were drinking in a dingy parlour, at the back of one of those public houses it is so difficult to find by daylight, within call of Leicester Square. It was eleven o'clock a.m., and they were testing the merits of gin and water as compared with gin and cloves, the Patron, it is unnecessary to observe, preferring the stronger compound. Jericho, dressed in a style he designated " bang-up," which caused him to look like a broken-down billiard-marker, insisted on standing treat, and the Patron, holding a pewter measure lately refilled, was enjoying that placid state of imbecility in which most of his hours were passed.

" She's a *good* gal," said he, "and a handsome, beautiful, and dutiful, free with her money too, like a real lady ; but I *could* wish as she'd bring herself to trust the old father a bit. She's

close, Jerry, that's what she is. It's hard to
think sometimes as she's my own child."

"There's her marks," observed the other.

"There's her marks," repeated Jack, smack-
ing his lips over the gin and cloves. "If it
weren't for her marks I'd swear on a book as
she'd been born a queen. Only to see her walk,
Jerry. Blessed if I know whether she *does* walk :
it's more like the sailing of a ship. And to think
that's my Shuri's babby, as kep' me awake crying, night after night, on Leatherhead Common,
under the stars. When I've got to die, Jerry,
please God I'll do it out o' doors."

His eye wandered, his tongue seemed growing large in his mouth ; the dreams of his youth,
and the cloves, and perhaps the gin, were too
much for him.

"I remember as if it was yesterday," he continued, shaking his head, "old Aunt Ryley she
came to supper in our tent, with a needle, and a
handful of gunpowder as she borrowed off of

poaching Jim Lovell. 'Name this child,' says
she. 'Shuri,' says I, 'for the little one is as like
her mother as a cygnet to a swan.' 'Not a bit
of it,' says my Shuri. 'We mustn't call it John,'
says she, 'because it's a lass; but we'll call it
Jane,' says she. 'Prick it in, Aunt Ryley,' says
she: 'J for Jane and L for Lee. That's as
near as we can get.' How it squeaked, poor
little beggar! And now they're all gone. Where,
Jerry? That's it. I wish as I know'd. Aunt
Ryley, and my Shuri, and plenty more, while
little Jane Lee grow'd into a real lady, gloves,
and a gold watch, and money in both pockets,
and a silk gownd on her back, and a slate roof
over her head. What's the meaning of it all,
Jerry? And how is it worked? That beats
me!"

But Jerry, who was not drunk enough to
embark on such visionary speculations, felt more
interest in the present prosperity of Mrs. Paravant, and the advantages he could derive there-

from, than in the future prepared for his whole nation. He questioned the Patron, therefore, pretty narrowly, on the income and belongings of this ornament to the tribe.

"For," said he, "it seems but fair as she should share and share alike with you and me. She's a Romany, whether or no: nothing can wash it out of her, not if she married a hundred Gorgios, and being a Romany, she must abide by Romany laws. She's broken one of the strictest already, and by rights she ought to be called to account."

"What!" exclaimed Jack, in a voice of thunder, that brought the potboy running into the room, when Jericho, with admirable presence of mind, ordered another measure of gin and cloves.

"Look ye here, my lad!" and the old boxer laid his formidable fist on the table: "there was a chap at Guilford Races, the Hero of Hexham, they called him in the ring, as up and spoke disrespectful of my Shuri. His pals had to lift him into a trap, and take him back to Hexham that same arternoon, and it wasn't a matter of three rounds at most. There was a swell, a lord of Parliament, he was, as tried to put an affront on my pretty, only t'other night in London streets. If ever he's come to again, he thinks as a horse kicked him, I know!

"Here's your health, Jerry: you're a honest lad, and you means well; but don't you let your tongue run too fast, a-jawin' about my lass. If you and me was to fall out, I might larn you a trick or two of the old trade, and it would be a bad job for both!"

So Jericho discreetly changed the subject, but none the less did he resolve, that whatever good fortune had befallen to his gipsy kins-woman, he would have his share.

CHAPTER XLIV.

WESTWARD HO!

AND now her very life became a burden to
Beltenebrosa under their exactions. The elder
claimed her time, the younger gipsy her money,
without scruple or apology, as a matter of right.
Old Jack was to be seen reeling up the pretty
staircase to the drawing-room floor every afternoon, with unfailing regularity, at the same hour
and in the same state; while Jericho, looking
thoroughly like a member of the swell mob in
his flash clothes and sham jewellery, wore his hat
in her presence, and smoked incessantly, without
the slightest regard to proprieties of time or
place. The landlady's manner grew suspicious-

—an elderly *gentlewoman*, as she called herself, on the ground floor, gave notice to quit; and even the servants treated their handsome lodger with less respect than when first she came into the house. They had been very proud of her then, boasting to small tradesmen, followers, and other associates, that she was a foreigner of noble extraction and boundless wealth. Now they wondered if a person who received such friends as Jack and Jericho could be barely respectable, anticipating a solution of the whole mystery at an early date before some worthy magistrate in Bow Street. But that she paid ready money, and always allowed herself to be systematically cheated out of small sums, a detective would have been called in long ago, to find, as usual, very little that he could detect; but even this questionable voucher seemed about to fail her, in consequence of the inroads made on her purse by the low extravagances of her gipsy kinsfolk. Jack, indeed, observed some limit in his demands, and so long as he had money enough in his pocket to treat a boon companion, and thoroughly moisten his own clay in a public house, troubled his daughter only with interminable maunderings about her mother and maudlin professions of affection for herself; but Jericho was not so easily satisfied, and had her modest hundreds been increased to thousands, it seemed that his repeated inroads would have exhausted them all.

Now he required such a suit of clothes from a fashionable tailor as should do justice to the good looks he was conscious of possessing; anon he could not do without a gold watch : all *gentlemen* wore them, and a gold watch, unlike other ornaments, was as good as a bank-note; it would fetch its price in sovereigns when he was obliged to put it " up the spout." Small change, too, of course he must have in his pockets. How could he refuse to treat a friend of either sex? A man must not forego the duties of his position; and Jericho talked, perhaps felt, as if he were really a person of property and character. Since his enlistment in the ranks of professional crime, as distinguished from the occasional dishonesty of a gipsy's life, he had found himself well supplied with ready money, and had contracted expensive tastes, foreign to his early habits, indeed, but extremely agreeable to his half-savage nature, which he grudged no effort to indulge. It seemed no part of his character to run unnecessary risk, and he was the last man to take the chance of imprisonment, particularly with hard labour, in the acquisition of funds, when he need only swagger up a flight of stairs into a lady's drawing-room, ask for what he wanted, and swagger down again. Such rogues never seem to realize the possibility of killing the goose with the golden eggs, of heaping feathers on the camel's back till it breaks; and he repeated the process over and over again, forgetting that no well is perfectly inexhaustible,

and it can only be a question of time how soon
the insatiable bucket comes up dry.

Beltenebrosa was now going through a process which most of us experience at one period
or another of our lives, out of which we ought
to come improved, and at any rate do come
somewhat sobered and reclaimed. According to
her lights, which were of the faintest—only a
glimmer, so to speak, through palpable darkness
—she was endeavouring to do right. Looking
back on her past life, how empty it seemed! how
aimless! how useless! The very prizes for which
she strove were so worthless when won! the
chaplets that crowned her such withered leaves
after all! What had she tried for? Happiness?
Yes; but did she ever attain it, or even a good
imitation of it? Not when she, the gipsy found-
ling, saw herself an object of envy and admiration among the great ones of the earth. Not on
that memorable day when she sat at a royal table,
and men who were making history in Europe vied

with each other to carry her parasol and shawl.
Not when she walked by the blue Mediter-
ranean with the young husband who, whatever
might have been his shortcomings, thought no
price too high for her approval and regard, nor
regretted for a moment to have offended relatives,
friends, neighbours, and all the prejudices he had
imbibed from childhood, to make her his own.
Not when she escaped with him from these very
kinsmen, who now so tormented her, in the
memorable ride on Potboy, that furnished keen
excitement and an enlivening sense of enterprise
—nothing more; not when she first tasted the
sweets of liberty and independence, leading the
life of a lady bachelor in the little street off Long
Acre; no, not even in that moment of triumph,
when she saw Mervyn Strange at her feet, and
the grave young clergyman, who with his body
worshipped her, with *half* his worldly goods did
her endow! While she looked in his honest
loving eyes, she was near the happiness she had

dreamed of for a short five minutes, but did not quite attain it even then.

There must have been something strangely amiss, she began to think, in the objects of her life, and its whole conduct, or she could not have been thus baffled in pursuit of a desire that eluded her so persistently from day to day and from year to year. She had not yet learned her lesson. She did not know that just as all great discoveries are made when science is looking for something else, and men blunder into truth as Columbus blundered into America, so those who seek after Happiness always fail to find her, while she comes of her own free will to visit him who is content to mate with Duty, sitting soberly at home.

Beltenebrosa entertained some vague notion that her legitimate task was to be performed in the care of her drunken old father and reprobate kinsman. It arose partly from a sense of natural affection, instinctive rather than intelligent, partly

from the dislike to solitude and the desire o
being necessary to somebody, which are such
essential attributes of the female character.

She tried hard to bear with both her tormentors, but gave way under the infliction.

One afternoon, old Jack being fast asleep
and helplessly drunk in the back drawing-room,
Jericho made his appearance, with a cigar in his
mouth, and a glossy hat, very much aslant, on
his head. He made no attempt to remove either
of these ornaments from respect to his hostess,
and sat himself down on her sofa in a free-and-
easy manner, which made her long that her
sturdy young husband could come back alive, if
only for five minutes, to kick him out.

" Sister," said he, knocking the ashes off his
cigar with a slender tawny over-ringed finger,
" I wants to have a bit of a chat with you. No,
I ain't going to ask for money this time,—not a
dump! But it's a matter of business too. I've
been thinking a good deal about *you* of late.

It's a rum thing. Sister, you come between me and my sleep."

"Well?" she asked, rising haughtily to her feet, roused by something in his manner to an impulse of anger and defiance that she could not control.

He jerked his thumb towards the next room, where Jack's snores could be heard rising and falling in sonorous regularity. "He's failing, sister," said Jericho; "the Patron's about done. He's on his last legs; he says so hisself. Now, it's on my mind, this is, and I can't shake it off nohow. Suppose as the Patron was to go under, what's to become of *you?*"

She stared at him in angry surprise. "*Become* of me!" she repeated. "I don't understand you. If anything should happen to—to my father I might perhaps go to Brighton for change of air, and of course I could not have *you* coming in and out at all hours; but that is the only difference it would make in my daily life."

"Steady!" he interrupted. "You talk big —very big. You seem to have forgotten——"

"Forgotten what?"

"Your marriage and its price. You haven't worked it out, sister. It's hanging over you now, the same as the first day you left me on my back in the heather to ride off with your Gorgio lover. It's bad enough to marry out of your tribe, but it's death—d'ye mind me?— *death* to marry out of your nation!"

"Nonsense! I've had enough of this. You can't frighten me any more with your old women's tales. You threaten freely, but you seem to forget that bloodshed is a game two may play at, and perhaps I can draw a trigger as easy as you can a knife."

His cheek blanched, and she marked his eye scan her dress and figure as if to see whether she carried a pistol concealed about her person.

The empty threat seemed to have cowed him.

He removed his hat, laid down his cigar, and continued in a more humble tone.

"There's no call for that, sister, so long as Jericho Lee can stand upright. I've watched over your safety, ah! much oftener than you think. I'd like to watch over it always. Sister, you've been a Gorgio's widow; will you come back to your people and be a Romany's wife? Now it's out. Give me an answer, yes or no."

She was speechless with indignation. In her most desponding moments she had never contemplated such a come-down as this. That Jericho was to be a tax on her resources, a recurring annoyance, an importunate beggar, to be alternately bought off and driven away—to this she was in a manner reconciled; but that he should presume to offer himself to her—*her*— the Beltenebrosa of last season—as a husband, was an insult so outrageous as to seem positively incredible even now.

She drew herself up, and her eyes fairly

blazed with anger while she replied, measuring
him from top to toe with glances of unspeakable
scorn,

"If you had asked for a place as *my footman*,
I should have said you were not tall enough, and
your character would not bear inquiry! To your
unheard-of impertinence I answer simply this,
that I recommend you to walk out by the door,
before the Patron wakes, or most assuredly you
will have to leave by the window!"

Then she marched like a queen into the next
room, where old Jack was sleeping, and locked
the door.

She did not see the dangerous scowl on
Jericho's face while he went downstairs into the
street by the safer route she had suggested; but
none the less did she resolve that the time had
come to put a stop to this persecution, once for
all. It had only needed some such climax as
the foregoing to bring matters to a head, and
with that promptitude for action which she in-

herited from her father, she decided on leaving
London immediately, and effectually giving her
gipsy friends the slip.

She kissed the old man's forehead as he lay
sleeping heavily on the sofa, and was surprised
at her own weakness. She made up a packet of
bank-notes, every shilling she could spare, and
thrust them into his pocket. She paid her rent,
and a week extra in lieu of notice, packed up
her things, sent for a cab, and was at Paddington Station before the Patron woke from his
drunken slumbers, or Jericho had thoroughly
digested the insult he considered himself to have
received.

She could not have explained, perhaps, why
she should travel by this particular railway out
of London, or analyse an instinct that impelled
her to fly for safety to the west, as some noble
red deer, hunted from his leafy haunts by horn
and hound, stretches across the glorious wilds of
Somerset and Devon, westward, westward still,

by combe and copse, boulder and bracken, rugged glen and russet moorland, till he makes his plunge for liberty and death, forty fathoms of sheer descent, into the Severn Sea.

Let us hope that the sufferings of the hunted are in no proportion to the keen engrossing pleasure enjoyed by those who hunt.

Beltenebrosa, to carry on the metaphor, harboured, found, and fairly forced into the open, determined to make her point. It was natural, perhaps, that she should fly to the other end of the kingdom; but why she selected Boarshaven as her city of refuge, I leave to be explained by those who are more versed than I am in the complicated mechanism of a woman's heart.

The town is dirty and over-populated; the streets are narrow, ill smelling, and ill paved; every third door seems to open on a slop-shop, every fourth on a public house. The inhabitants are an amphibious race, never by any chance clean, though constantly wet through: the men wear Guernsey frocks, with high canvas trousers, and the shortest of cotton braces; the women, limp stuff dresses of a neutral tint, that cling so helplessly about the figure as to forbid the idea of there being anything but the wearer underneath. Forests of masts, rising from brigs and schooners, look as if they grew in the very streets. There is no sand nor shingle, but abundance of mud, and all the smells of a sea-port rest in the atmosphere, except the free salt air of ocean itself.

"First to Boarshaven; single." She wondered whether she would ever come back even while she took her ticket, but concerned herself little about her boxes, which a stalwart porter, diligent in the service of well-dressed ladies travelling alone, and good for shillings—certain, when he put them in their compartments after duly labelling, was wheeling to the platform, because she was too much engaged in speculating on the result of this new step. She had opened, so to speak, a fresh volume in the history of her life: was it to be eventful? had it a hero? and how would it end?

Though accustomed to admiration, and pre-occupied besides about her future, she did not yet fail to notice that she had made a great impression on a diminutive youth, conspicuous for an extremely tall hat, who was lounging about the purlieus of the station, as if waiting for a train. This little personage, with his pale cockney face and sharp twinkling eyes, seemed of a very observant nature, and found in Beltenebrosa an object that riveted his whole attention from the moment she entered the booking-office. Never in his life had he beheld such a woman, and he felt he could not admire her enough! He was at her side while she took her ticket, he followed her to the carriage when she got in, he saw her give the porter a shilling and buy a *Punch* of the newsboy, and, as she glided smoothly away from the platform, rejoicing that she was outward bound at last, he stared after her, open-mouthed, with an imbecile expression, that much belied his native cunning, on his pale face, and his tall hat pushed to the very back of his head.

CHAPTER XLV.

MAHOGANY PARLOUR.

A NARROW room with sanded floor, divided into
boxes by high wooden partitions; tables and
benches worn and stained with use; a low roof,
windows well shuttered and secured, so as to
keep out the slightest breath of air; articles of
property, such as baskets, shawls, handkerchiefs,
and great-coats, lying about so carelessly as to
verify the proverb that there is "honour among
thieves;" a smell of ardent spirits pervading the
atmosphere; and a potman moving through clouds
of tobacco-smoke, with shirt sleeves rolled to the
shoulders, and long sinewy arms, that looked as

if they could hit out with the force of a catapult:
"The Kangaroo," though a light-weight, is no
contemptible bruiser, and an ugly customer in
more senses than one.

This haunt is called by its frequenters "Mahogany Parlour," not because its furniture is con-
structed of that imperishable substance, as might
naturally be supposed, but on account of a certain drink that first came into vogue here with
the swell mob, introduced by a travelled gentleman, who had learned to appreciate its merits in
the New World. Gin and treacle, mixed in due
proportion, under the name of "Mahogany," is
a compound that finds favour with the "lum-
berers" of Canada and the Western States, men
who live hard and athletic lives, felling and floating timber in primeval forests for nine months
of the year, and spend the other three in drink
and dissipation in the Settlements.

It agreed better, perhaps, with these stalwart
heroes than with the London thieves, a puny

race, relying on cunning more than courage, and skill of brain rather than strength of arm.

Fighting Jack, who was, so to speak, an honorary member of this select society, tolerated for his personal prowess, but labouring under the disadvantage of comparative honesty, could drink "Mahogany" or anything else; but Jack was seldom able to form a distinct idea now, and, whether his gin had or had not been adulterated with treacle, consumed so much as to render him helpless of body and utterly idiotic of mind.

Waking up in her back drawing-room to find no daughter and a bundle of bank-notes in his pocket, he brought his intellects to bear on such a coincidence with considerable difficulty, but managed to infer that she must have gone away for a definite period, and that his best plan would be to consult Jericho on their future proceedings without delay. So he staggered off to "Mahogany Parlour," where he found, as he expected, his kinsman and prime adviser smoking cigars, while treating two fair companions to some execrable champagne. Of this beverage Jack was *not* drunk enough to partake, but desiring The Kangaroo to place some undiluted spirits on another table, he drew his kinsman aside, and imparted the startling information with which he was charged.

Jerry had plenty of self-command. The scowl of rage, spite, and disappointment that passed like a shadow over his dark, good-looking, bad-looking face vanished with the mouthful of spirits he swallowed to soothe his vexation, and he observed calmly, "I suppose as you didn't think of following of her, or taking of the number of her cab, or getting anyways on her track?"

"How could I do that?" expostulated the other; "didn't I tell ye as I was resting on the sofy, and someway I think I must have been asleep—a kind of dog-sleep, you know. But she can't be gone fur, and if you thinks, Jerry, as she'd be taking a ride in a cab or suchlike, why, we've as good as got our hand on her. I knows lots of cabmen, bless ye, and every man on 'em would be willing to do me a turn. I'm about told out, Jerry, but there's here and there a one yet as respects old Jack!"

The younger gipsy reflected. To embark on a search or any other undertaking requiring common prudence with the Patron would be to ensure failure. Mind and body, the old boxer was indeed on his last legs, and Jericho bethought him, with an evil smile, how much more promising would be his own future when no longer hampered by the companionship of this worn-out kinsman, with his addled brains, incautious tongue, stubborn courage, and inconvenient notions regarding right and wrong.

"His money would pretty nigh set me up," thought Jericho, speculating, though he was only a gipsy, how his senior would "cut up" with as little scruple as if he had been a Christian gentleman of birth and education: "he can't have pulled out less than twenty pounds in notes when he paid for his gin.. Twenty pounds! It would come in very handy! And as for the old man, I could do better without him. He's fit for nothing now. Every dog has his day!"

So he plied Jack with more liquor, pressing him to drink with the ladies he had just left, whose voices were to be heard rising in loud shrill laughter as the champagne mounted to their brains, and seated him between them like Macheath in the "Beggars' Opera," well satisfied with his position. Then Jerry lighting another cigar, pondered how he was to get on the track of Mrs. Paravant, and hunt her down once more.

"I was allus a ladies' man," said a voice in the adjoining box, which he had no difficulty in recognizing as that of a promising young pick-pocket with whom he had done business some weeks ago, whose diminutive size and extreme self-assumption had earned him the nickname of Buster; "but I never see such a one-er! Dress!

o' course she was dressed 'andsome : black, I tell
ye, plain and genteel, with the gloss on, fresh out
of a mourning warehouse, I know. But there!
it wasn't her dress as fetched *me*. Them two in
the next box is *dressed* 'andsome enough ; but
you might as well talk of twopenn'orth of ginger
pop alongside of a bottle of cham' ! "

"Did you speak to her ? " asked a pale, un-
happy-looking girl, for whose edification this
pocket hero seemed to be holding forth.

"Well, I did *not* speak to her, Molly, and
that's the truth," replied Buster. "I ain't easy
dashed, 'specially with the women, as *you* knows,
Molly. But, someway, this here looked like a
queen, and there—I dursn't ! So pale she was,
and so tall, with her hair as black as jet, and eyes
that flashed like a pair of candles. I'll tell you
what, Molly : if a red-nosed chap had gone for to
kiss her, I think they'd have blowed his head
off ! "

Molly, a fair, undersized girl, who would have

looked washed-out but that she was so dirty,
seemed restlessly inclined to change the subject;
but Jericho, overhearing his young friend's glowing description, began to think it just possible so
transcendent a beauty might be the very person
whose destination he wanted to find out.

"My service to you," said he, politely offer-
ing to "stand" any beverage they fancied, as
he leaned over this young couple in their box.
—"What! he's been at his old games, has he,
Miss? Ah, he's a good judge, is Buster. I said
so myself the first Sunday I see him walking out
with *you*."

Poor Molly smiled, and Buster, emptying his
glass, performed a most conceited wink.

"That's wot I was a-tellin' her," said he; "but
bless ye! there was no mistake about the stunner
I seen to-day. If I thought as she'd ever come
back, blowed if I wouldn't rent one of them large
houses opposite Paddington Station, and live in
the first-floor front."

"Paddington Station," repeated Jericho, dreading lest an inflection of his voice should betray his interest, and speaking as carelessly as he could. "Oh! that's where you goes wife-hunting, is it? I suppose you wouldn't take *me* with you to-morrow, just for a show! there's no harm in looking, you know."

The other grinned. "'Taint no use," said he, "she's far enough by now; I seen her ticket. First-class, I tell ye. Oh! a real lady, no mistake about that. If I hadn't been short of small change, just for once in a way, blessed if I wouldn't have gone with her. But it's a matter of two quid to Boarshaven, and I'd got nothing in my pocket but threeha'porth o' coppers, and a pewter half-crown as I took in this werry parlour. So I'll have to do with Molly here, and the other, she'll have to do without *me!*"

"Boarshaven's a long way," observed Jerry, with an unmoved countenance. "'Tother end of nowheres. I fancy you're a sight more comfort-

able here; better company, too. Good evening,
Buster! good evening, Miss! Don't you let
him go to Paddington Station no more!"

So Jericho took his leave, followed by the
admiring glances of these young people, who
considered him a vastly agreeable man, of
polished manners, rising to the top of his profession.

Notwithstanding his confidence in Buster's
quick eye and correct taste, he resolved to verify
that observer's account by an immediate visit to
Paddington Station, whilst the events of the day
were fresh in the minds of such officials as he
knew how to cross-examine, with the assistance
of a few pleasant words and a drop of beer. If,
as he suspected, Mrs. Paravant had fled for safety
to a remote and obscure refuge, he would follow
in due time, that is to say, as soon as he was out
of funds; meanwhile he would give old Jack
the slip, temporarily, while he prosecuted his
researches,—perhaps permanently, when he had

resolved on some definite course. Friendless
and unprotected, the courage that had sustained
his prey must give way at last, and the next time
he asked, perhaps she might look less contemp-
tuously on his suit.

Jerry's own experience of women had taught
him that violent outbursts of anger often fade
to unconditional surrender and collapse; but, he
told himself at the same time, he had no fancy
for such "breezes," and that his personal courage
was unequal to so keen an encounter as he had
that day sustained.

CHAPTER XLVI.

OUTWARD BOUND.

THE Patron, sitting between his fair companions, seemed quite satisfied with his position, and though not strictly handsome, nor attired in the best taste, their manners were lively and accommodating, while any superfluous energy of speech or gesture might be attributed to the champagne, of which, having already partaken freely, they were persuaded to share another bottle. The Kangaroo, indeed, who brought it, seemed to regard the whole proceeding with covert displeasure, intimating as much in dumb show, that Jack was too far gone to mark or compre-

hend. This young pugilist entertained for the
famous veteran feelings of mingled envy and admiration; he scanned with emotion the wreck of
that finely-built form, which had come victorious
out of one of the gamest battles ever fought in
the ring. He would have given a crown to see
the old hero strip, a pound and more to put the
gloves on with him, not to contend,—far be it
from him!—but to watch his attitudes in all
humility and respect. He regarded him much
as the soldiers of the first Napoleon did Marshal
Ney, or as we used, forty years ago, to regard
the great Duke of Wellington.

Of the ladies who supported his idol at
either side, he had the lowest opinion; believing
them, not without reason, capable of picking his
hero's pocket, to leave him drunk and helpless
in the street. It seemed impossible, however, to
impart such an opinion to Jack, who was fast
attaining his usual state, and the Ganymede of
this Olympus had, besides, quite enough on his

own hands in the matter of supplying·orders and scrutinizing small change.

A final glass of gin, neat and sparkling, settled his business at last, and the old gipsy sank forward between his fair supporters, fast asleep, against the table, with his head on his crossed arms.

Said one of the free companions, in a whisper that was only to be interpreted by the movement of her lips, " Share and share alike ? "

" Honour ? " returned the other below her breath.

" Right ! " was the reply, with the faintest symptoms of a wink ; and no further explanation seemed required.

" It won't do here, though," murmured the first speaker, glancing suspiciously round. " There's Redhead watching like a cat at a mouse-hole."

" Redhead be blowed ! " answered her " lady friend," as she called her, an impulsive and plain-spoken young woman. "If I'd been missis here, and I might have been too, Susan, if I'd thought well, that there Kangaroo would have had the key of the street three months ago. I wish he was dead, I do!"

"It's no use wishing," replied Susan, who seemed a practical person enough, except in the matter of dress, "nor talking neither. Wot's o'clock, my dear? I think I could relish a cup of strong black tea; bitter strong," she added, sinking her voice; "and that will sober him for a time if anything can, and we wouldn't want to keep him long."

So the strong black tea was brought, and Fighting Jack, with a good deal of pushing and pinching, was roused to partake of it, when he recovered sufficiently to stand on his legs and leave the thieves' haunt, supported by these two ladies, who expressed a charitable intention of seeing him home. The Kangaroo looked wistfully after his retreating figure, and shook his head.

The night was mild, with a soft west wind blowing, that even in the purlieus of Leicester Square breathed cool and fresh on Jack's throbbing temples and heated face. But the open air soon mollified the sobering effects of tea, and his guides found no little difficulty in steering their charge from lamp-post to lamp-post. He was a heavy man still, and lurched forward, ever and anon, with a sway that nearly sent all three to the ground, and they laughed, of course, and chattered incessantly, but held on like grim death the while. Presently Susan plunged her hand in his pocket, to abstract three five-pound notes, a few sovereigns, and some loose silver, half of which plunder, as she protested, and indeed swore, she tendered her companion, on the spot.

"We've done with the old bloke now," said she; "and the sooner we makes our lucky, the better! Take care, Carrie! we mustn't let go, not both at once, or he'll never keep on his jolly old legs. Good night, my dear; you and me had best not be seen together. Good night!"

In spite of her precautions, however, and though deprived, by judicious degrees, of his charming supports, old Jack seemed quite unable to steer his own course without assistance, and bumped heavily against a lamp-post to which he clung, looking about him in perfect good-humour and content.

Susan was round the corner and half-way to her miserable home in the twinkling of an eye, well satisfied with her share of the robbery, which amounted to three-fourths of the whole sum purloined. Caroline, on the contrary, commonly called The Shiner, from her bright apparel, could not forbear hovering round their victim a little longer, with certain instincts of womanly compunction that, unsexed as it was, still remained in her weak, depraved, unhappy heart.

Like Hood's ruined Magdalen, shivering at the door of the palace where her destroyer feasted

with his friends, it might have been said of poor
Caroline—

"She who now shrinks from the wintry weather,
    Ah! she once had a village fame;
Listened to love on the moonlit heather,
    Had gentleness, vanity, maiden shame."

Youth, innocence, and happiness had faded
in a past that The Shiner tried hard to forget,
succeeding, to tell the truth, in haunts of vice
for many hours at a time; but do what she
would, memory persisted in tormenting her on
occasions, and none knew better than herself
how sad and solitary was the so-called gaiety of
the life she led.

"I can't let the old man lie in the street,"
thought this miserable Samaritan. "He's no
more able to take care of himself than a babby
at the breast. And them peelers, if they runs
him in, they'll have no mercy. Likely as not,
leave him upside down in the stone jug till
morning. Then he'll die, and I'll see him every

night in my sleep. I wish I'd never come nigh
here; I wish I hadn't touched his money; I
wish I'd let the whole jolly business be. Ah!
if we gets to wishing, I wish I'd never been
born!"

Then she returned to the gipsy, detached
him from his lamp-post, and although her own
lair was in a contrary direction, supported his
wavering steps towards the West-end.

Her nerves were weak. How could they be
otherwise in the life she led? And the conduct
of her charge tried them severely. Though some
animal instinct, such as leads a dying wolf to its
den, guided him homewards, old Jack's head
was quite gone. All along Piccadilly he rambled
in his talk, as though delirious from fever rather
than drink; not that he was violent, indeed, nor
offensive in any way, but wholly beside himself,
and unconscious of his surroundings. By degrees, as his mind failed, his step grew firmer,
and his bodily vigour seemed to return. When

they reached Hyde Park he left his companion's arm to walk on unassisted, and made shift to explain he was well able to take care of himself.

" But thank ye kindly, Miss," observed Jack, with great politeness, and some hazy notion that his guide, in common propriety, ought to accompany him no farther. " Our way lies apart now, very wide apart, young woman, or I'd ask you home to take a cup o' tea or what not, in the camp. But I'm married, my lass, though you wouldn't think it, and my Shuri she's not best pleased when I've been on the burst for a bit, like this here, unless I comes home alone. You'll excuse *me*, my dear, but it's best to speak the truth when you've got to do with women. I wish you good night, kindly, Miss. You make the best of your way home : there's some precious scamps about ; but if any of them offers to say anything to you, don't you be dashed ; you speak up, and tell 'em Fighting Jack—that's me, my dear—isn't regular out of the ring yet. They haven't forgot, never fear! And look ye, my lass, I ain't got no watch on me—I put mine up the spout last week—but I ought to have a matter of seventeen or eighteen quid in my pocket. I'm trying to find it now. You're welcome to it all—all—free! You'd maybe want to get back to your friends. Ah! you'd be better at home than in this here town. But spend it to please yourself. What am I, to advise the like of you? Dash it all! I'm such a heedless chap! I must have dropped it somewheres!"

Caroline's heart smote her, the tears were running down her wasted cheeks. She produced her share of the stolen property, and pressed it into his reluctant hand.

"Take it," said she, sobbing; "it's your own, every brass farden of it! And—and—don't think bad of me. I wasn't always a gay woman. I was a good girl once."

He put it away from him with a strange smile, and either the gaslight deceived her or

there was the look in his eyes of one who sees
something a long way off.

"Bless ye, it's no use to *me!*" he answered.
"Why, the battle-money's got to be paid to-
night, and I shall have a sight more than I can
spend. Besides, my dear, I shan't want for
nothing where I'm a-goin ; there's plenty for all
—men, women, and little barelegged children—
and never a mag to pay! Commons stretching
as far as you can see, with the furze-bloom
shining on 'em, and dazzling like gold, and the
blue sky coming right down to the ground on
every side, without stack or chimney, or so much
as a barn, to spoil the view. Woods with sticks
for the gathering, hen-pheasants, rabbits, and a
fallow buck or two, as tame as goats. Streams,
my dear, with trout leaping up into the sunshine, and pools you can see the fish basking in,
like shadows of their own selves, always fat and
always hungry. I've a tent of my own under an
oak, the biggest tree in the whole blessed forest,

and a kettle that simmers all day long, and
they're only waiting to begin supper till the Patron
comes home. There's the lads and lasses, I can
see them plain enough—fine, wiry, active young
chaps !—black-browed girls, as straight as willow
wands, bringing the firewood in and skimming
the pot, so as you can smell the stew a mile off !
All for old Jack !—all against the Patron comes
home ! And—yes ! I knowed it ! There she is,
standing out in front, shading her eyes with her
hand—my Shuri, as beautiful as a queen, wondering what has kept me so long—looking, longing,
wearing to see her own old Fighting Jack again.
What a lot we'll have to say to each other !
We're not used to be parted, her and me; but
that's done with now. My Shuri ! I'm never
a-going to leave you no more. Good night,
Miss, I can't stop no longer; but I'll tell my
Shuri how polite you was to her old man,
helping of him along the road, and precious
rough it were, till you brought him to the end.

I'll not forget. Thank you kindly, Miss, and
good night!"

She was terribly frightened, yet loth to let
him walk on by himself, thus lost to all realities,
through the darkness of the Park, into which he
insisted on plunging, affirming that it was the
nearest way to the camp he seemed so desirous
to reach.

"Won't you think better of it?" she expostulated. " Let you and me keep in the street where
there's light. We knows the ins and outs there;
but you can't dodge a peeler with a bullseye
under them trees in the dark.''

" Peeler!" repeated the old prize-fighter,
clenching his fist. "I'd like to see the best
peeler as ever wore a hat offer to come between
me and my Shuri. I'd spoil him so as his inspector wouldn't never know him no more. But
I can't spare the time to stand talking here all
night. Once again, Miss, I wish you good
evening."

She nerved herself for a final effort, and deserved as much credit for valour as the hero who leads a storming party.   Probably the one thing she most dreaded on earth was to be alone at midnight with a madman in Hyde Park; but she resolved to risk it.

"Take me with you," she urged. "I've come a long walk.   I'm tired to death, and you can't refuse to give me shelter."

He passed his hand over her forehead with a gesture that seemed like a blessing. "It's not to be done, my dear," he answered, kindly. "You couldn't come where I'm a-going. Maybe you wouldn't want to if you knowed."

And with a wave of his powerful arm, that seemed to forbid any attempt at following, he walked away steadily through the Park gates into the night.

CHAPTER XLVII.

"HAVE I FOUND THEE, O MINE ENEMY?"

LORD ST. MORITZ as a valetudinarian! It provoked him exceedingly; he hated to be told of it; but the doctor and his own feelings warned him that unless he began to take care of himself. he might become a confirmed invalid for life! He had always acted on the principle that nature is our best guide, and doubtless, under certain severe restrictions, this may be a sufficiently wise rule for the preservation of health; but it must not be adopted according to his Lordship's interpretation, that whatever you fancy is sure to do you good. Eat when you are hungry, certainly, but not four courses and a dessert. Drink also when thirsty, but less than a bottle of dry champagne and another of loaded claret at the same meal; while anybody who smokes as much as he feels inclined must necessarily consume a great deal more tobacco than is good for his nerves or digestion. Amusement, too, though excellent when taken sparingly, is not half so healthy a tonic in excess as hard work; and an over-dose of it, acting through the brain, brings on that sense of mental and bodily prostration which society has consented to particularize by the term " bored."

This is a state to which, like some epidemics, those are most liable who hold it in the greatest horror, and Lord St. Moritz all his life had certainly taken pains to avoid the slightest symptoms of the disease. Nevertheless, even his Lordship was but mortal, and found himself at last not only ailing in health and weakened by infirmity, but exceedingly bored with the remedial treatment he was compelled to undergo. It was no wonder he failed at last; even such a constitution as his could not but succumb to many consecutive years of good living, late hours, excitement, dissipation, and unscrupulous self-indulgence, followed up by an encounter with a professed pugilist, in which he had sustained a blow that might have felled an ox. He did not leave his room for a week, nor visit his club for a fortnight; and even when all outward marks of the brawl had disappeared, felt that his whole system was shaken and his digestion completely upset. The accident, as he chose to call it, fortunately occurred in the hunting season, so that inquiries could be parried by the usual explanation, "a bad fall." The most officious of friends, justly dreading detailed accounts of such a catastrophe, pursued their researches no further; but with his doctor he was obliged to be more candid, and that sage, though he smiled hopefully, pronounced no decided opinion, but shook his head.

"We must be careful," protested the medicine man. "We must avoid late hours, fatigue, unnecessary excitement. No, he should not recommend the sea; what we required was perfect quiet, and freedom from exertion of mind or body. We must avoid annoyance, vexation of any kind; and parliamentary or other duties had better be postponed for some weeks. We should eat plain nourishing food, at regular hours, little and often. Yes, sound old wine, certainly; two or three glasses—no more; but a cigar could not prudently be allowed. Early rising would be most beneficial, and a walk, weather permitting, every morning before breakfast. Such a treatment, and the prescription, would soon set us on our legs again. When?—Ah! that was impossible to promise, but before very long, and— Thank you; yes, another visit about the same hour to-morrow."

Then the doctor bowed himself out, smooth, polite, smiling, and went to attend Mrs. Strip-

well, who was quite well, parrying with considerable tact the inquiries made by that lady concerning his Lordship's constitution, ailments, and
general habits of life.

Not having seen him since his mysterious
disappearance from the theatre, when he left her
in charge of " poor Algy," curiosity, with a spice
of pique, had so tormented her, that she mistook
it for a softer feeling ; and being one of those
ladies who prefer what they have *not* to what
they have, she entertained a romantic notion of
obtaining access to the patient in the disguise of
a nurse, and ministering to his wants till he got
well. She did not put it in practice, for many
reasons : she hated quiet, she hated trouble, she
hated everything but amusement, and a sick-room
bored her to death.

By calling in the same doctor, however, who
was a pleasant-spoken person and a great favourite with ladies, she secured half an hour's delightful gossip, and the latest particulars of his

interesting patient, with the certainty that her
inquiries would be duly reported to him at the
next visit. All this was cheap at a sovereign,
and Lord St. Moritz had not been confined to
his room eight-and-forty hours before Mrs. Stripwell began to fancy her liver was torpid, her
lungs were touched, her nerves affected, and her
whole system wanted tone, which could only be
restored by medical advice at least once a day.

Among other particulars she learned that
Lord St. Moritz was ordered to walk before
breakfast, and she actually proposed doing such
violence to her habits as to get out of bed at
daybreak, that she might meet him by chance,
and share with him this distasteful discipline.
So her maid called her at seven o'clock for three
consecutive mornings, till the effort was found to
be impossible, and the project had to be given
up.

Nevertheless, though it is a penance for man
or woman to rise before the accustomed time,

and for the former to shave by candlelight, an
early walk in Hyde Park is not without its reward. The air seems *cleaner*, as it is fresher,
than at any other period of the twenty-four
hours ; and if there should be a touch of hoar-
frost, such as often succeeds a mild winter's
night, much beauty, enhanced by the accompany-
ing mist, not fog, is to be admired in every
branch and twig of the leafless trees, magnified
to twice their natural size by a coating of con-
densed dew, like the sugar on the ornaments of
a wedding-cake in a confectioner's shop.

Lord St. Moritz, swinging along by the Ser-
pentine at the rate of four miles an hour, well
wrapped up, and glowing with that convalescence
which, perhaps from the force of contrast, seems
even more enjoyable than health, began to think
the world was not such a bad place after all, and
Hyde Park, though he seemed to have it pretty
well to himself, no unpleasant resort at eight a.m.
on a winter's day.

There were comparatively few of his fellow-creatures about, but he took the more note of those he saw. A squadron of the Life Guards on watering order filed leisurely past him at a walk. The good black troopers, with their rough coats on, looked smaller than usual under their lengthy riders, who bestrode them barebacked, longing during this coldest of parades for the warmth of stable duties, and subsequent consolation of the pipe. Then a brougham rolled speedily by, and inside, smoking a cigarette, in a brown "Ulster," he recognized a friend on his way (per rail) to hunt with the Rothschilds in the Vale of Aylesbury, forty miles off, to return again at night. For a moment, in anticipation of the excellent day's sport this enthusiast was almost sure to enjoy, he wished to accompany him; but presently reflected that the fences were somewhat stiff, and the ground deep, in the Land of Grass, where he was bound; that Mentmore stags had a perverse tendency to run straight in an opposite direction from their home; that twenty miles back to the station with a tired horse, followed· by forty more on a railway, possibly wet through, was inconsistent with his ideas of happiness, and that altogether he could spend his day more pleasantly in London.

Meantime, his friend, who loved a hunt, good, bad, or indifferent, better than any amusement on earth, had finished his cigarette and was out of sight. After this, he met a telegraph-boy with a worsted comforter round his neck, bearer, no doubt, of some important message, loitering to throw stones at the ducks, followed by a plainly-dressed, modest-looking, brown-haired girl, who could only be a daily governess. She walked fast and well: she looked bright, happy, and good. One moment some evil spirit whispered that she might prove a pleasant acquaintance; the next, his better angel told him he ought to be ashamed of himself; and his Lordship strode off in another direction, where the mist hung lower and the grass grew thicker, towards breakfast and home.

"What a beast the fellow is to be so drunk at this time in the morning!" he thought, as he came upon the prostrate figure of a man, lying face downwards, with a coating of white frost still unmelted on his broad motionless back. His Lordship's first impulse was to pass by, as did the priest and the Levite, on the other side; but a strange instinctive horror came over him like a chill, with the certain foreboding that what he saw stretched out there, stark and quiet, he must no longer call *him,* but *it!* He ran in, nevertheless, readily enough, though he knew it was too late, to turn the figure over on its back with some difficulty, for it was large and heavy, and he himself encumbered with a great-coat. Then he loosened the handkerchief round its neck, unclasped the rigid hands, which had turned a yellowish-grey already, and exclaimed,

"No use! no use! the man must have been dead for hours."

He spoke louder than he intended, for the exclamation brought to his side a policeman, looming very large through the mist, who, recognizing his Lordship for a gentleman, dismisses from his mind certain crude notions of hocussing, robbery, and a well-dressed ruffian, which had crossed it with the first glimpse he caught of the situation.

"What's up here?" he asked, sternly enough, but added, with a finger to his helmet, "I'm afraid, sir, as it's all over with the party. This man will never move a finger no more. You're not a medical gentleman, be you, sir?" for his comprehensive mind had already taken in the official report, coroner's inquest, and nature of the evidence.

"Not I," answered the other; "I wish I were. But all the doctors in London can do him no good."

"Right you are!" replied the policeman. "Look here, sir," and he pointed to the frozen dews on the hair and face of the corpse: "this man has been cold since daybreak."

Lord St. Moritz started: scanning the calm fixed face, with its firm jaw and grizzled eyebrows, the truth flashed upon him. It was indeed his old antagonist, the prize-fighter, who had mauled him so severely, but for whose rough usage he would not now have been walking in Hyde Park at this early hour. He owed him a turn, he had often told himself of late, and it would go hard but he should find means to pay the score! Yes, he had earnestly wished to meet his enemy again, but not like this!

Fighting Jack looked very calm and peaceful: the lines, worn in his rugged old face by age and dissipation, were already modified and softened under the beautifying touch of death. The smile with which he had set out to meet his

Shuri seemed carved round his rigid lips, and the fine frame, stretched in its ample proportions while they searched him for papers or other clue to his identity, looked worthy of some warlike Eastern king, slain in the forefront of battle, with bow and spear in hand.

It is needless to observe that poor old Jack's pockets had been stripped to the lining. And Lord St. Moritz was able to afford but little of the information required.

" I've seen him before," he said, incautiously.

" Where ? " asked the policeman, "and when did you see him last? you're not obliged to tell me, if you haven't a mind."

" In a street row," answered his Lordship, turning rather red. " It's some time ago ; but I haven't recovered the blow he dealt me yet."

The policeman pondered. " He must have been a strongish chap," he murmured, scanning the fine proportions of the corpse. " I'll have to trouble you for your address, sir," he added, in a louder tone. "Your evidence will likely be wanted on the inquest."

The other handed him his card, on reading which the policeman's manner became at once less suspicious and more respectful.

"I don't expect as it will be a troublesome job, my Lord," said he, with a judicial and encouraging air: "no fears, I should say, of an open verdict in this here case."

"Then you don't think there's been foul play, though his pockets *are* empty?"

"No, my Lord, I don't. He was very powerful, was this man. You can see that for yourself. There's not many could have stood up to him when it come to blows. He'd have cut up rough, this man, if they'd a-tried it on; and I observe no marks of violence, neither about his person nor on the grass. No, my Lord; I don't seem to see as this here could have been a case of foul play."

"Apoplexy, then?" suggested his Lordship, who wanted to get home to breakfast.

"You know best, my Lord," answered the policeman, lifting the helmet from his honest square head. "In my opinion, it's the visitation of God."

CHAPTER XLVIII.

"I SAY NOTHING."

MRS. TREGARTHEN, so she lived to boast, whatever might be her shortcomings as a Christian, did her duty as a wife, keeping her husband's house in plenty, respectability, and comfort, under the best possible management. Taking charge of her own stores, much to the dissatisfaction of successive cooks, who came and went like the slides of a magic lantern, she replenished her shelves at certain stated epochs, about the period of quarter-day. Once in three months it was this good lady's practice to proceed in great pomp, by railway and subsequent fly, to the town of Boarshaven, where she made sundry purchases more useful than ornamental, lunched with keen appetite, and returned afterwards home to dinner, more dictatorial than usual, but, as she always declared, "fagged to death, and utterly worn-out."

It was held a reproach to the Reverend Silas, who accompanied her on these occasions, that he should be wholly useless and inefficient—considered by servants and tradespeople a perfect nonentity in all domestic affairs; but this seemed a little unjust, inasmuch as she repudiated his assistance, when offered, with contumely and scorn. It was a sight to see her sailing down Ship Street, a narrow thoroughfare ill adapted for the passage of such first-raters, in an impossible bonnet and gown of many colours, with glaring gloves, a striped parasol, and double gold eye-glasses—now patronizing a tradesman, now bowing to an acquaintance; anon, addressing a few admonitory sentences to the rector, dragging rather wearily in the rear.

Certain squalid lanes—narrow, dark, and un-
inviting—debouch into Ship Street; and round
the corner of one, who should bounce, into the
very arms of his rector's wife, progressing in all
her glory, but their former curate—Mervyn
Strange!

It does not much signify what a man has
done—nobody can have presence of mind to cut
him at such short notice as this. The rector was
unaffectedly glad to see his friend : shook hands,
and told him so. Mrs. Tregarthen was completely taken aback—could not but follow suit,
and in five minutes the three were marching
under the gateway of the old-established " Bull
and Bootjack," where luncheon awaited them, as
if they were the staunchest allies in the world.
That this meal should be served in the apartment occupied by poor James Paravant when he
carried off his gipsy bride, would have seemed a
more remarkable coincidence, had the hotel
boasted another sitting-room. As it was, Mrs.

Tregarthen set her bonnet straight, and contemplated the increasing redness of her nose in the
same mirror that reflected the very different
features of Beltenebrosa scarcely a year and a
half ago. The rector's wife, however, was no
less convinced of her good looks than of her
good appetite, and took her place at table in a
temper more convivial, a flow of spirits more
genial than usual.

The meal, which seemed principally to consist of strong cheese, a great many glasses, and
some gigantic celery, was brought in by an
apple-faced parlour-maid, who, knowing the
tastes of her customers, promptly, and without
orders, supplied two tumblers of port-wine negus,
while she placed before Mervyn Strange, after
some hesitation, a modest jug of small beer.

So long as this industrious person bustled
about the room, conversation was general, very
general indeed, turning on the ministrations of
the Church, the filthy state of the town, the in-

clemency of the weather, and such safe topics, carrying no personal import or allusion; but when she departed, and the negus began to act, Mrs. Tregarthen could refrain no longer: the fire burned within her, and she spoke with her lips.

"You haven't asked about any of your old friends," said she, with a meaning nod. "That's not like *you*. I never thought you were one of the out-of-sight out-of-mind sort."

He had left off blushing long ago: he had no time for such frivolities; but he murmured something unintelligible about the rheumatics of Goody This and the gout of Farmer That, to elicit from Mrs. Tregarthen a malicious laugh.

"Is there nobody you can think of," asked the rector's wife, stirring her negus, "that you were once interested in? No young lady who put herself under your charge, and gave you the slip at the first opportunity? You needn't kick me under the table, Silas. He has a right to

know.   What should you say, Mr. Strange, if I
told you that Jane Lee went away to be married ? "

What should he say?   What *had* he said
night after night in his prayers, but that he im-
plored she might be happy, and he might forget
her?   Married, indeed!   Had he not read the
service of his Church over her beautiful head,
with a sore and heavy heart?   Married!   This
loyal and true gentleman knew it only too well,
but he answered with as much composure as he
might,

    " Really, Mrs. Tregarthen?   Oh, indeed!"

    " Yes, married, Mr. Strange.   And more than
that, a widow into the bargain; but I'm sadly
afraid what they call a widow bewitched!   You
saw poor young Paravant's death in the papers,
—that shocking accident, you remember, at
Swansdown.   We dined at Combe-Wester the
very night before it happened, and who should
sit at the top of the table, as bold as brass, but

your precious Jane Lee, calling herself by some outlandish name, with all the airs and graces of a queen!"

"My dear, she did the honours remarkably well," interposed the rector. "She would have made poor James a good wife, if he had lived."

"Rubbish!" answered his lady. "Good wife, indeed! Much *you* know about good wives! You've had one for years, and never found it out. I tell you, she was his ruin. She'd have ruined a dozen such. Carriages, horses, new furniture, hothouse flowers, a French cook, and champage running like water. It's a mercy the young man did die, in my opinion, though it's my belief she was to blame for that too!"

"But she was fond of him, was she not?" asked the curate, wondering why his heart beat while he waited for an answer.

"Fond of him? yes, and fifty others! How poor James allowed it I can't think, only none

are so blind as those who *won't* see. Lords and
what not down from London, fashionable riff-
raff, and, as the Marchioness herself said, the
slang aristocracy. Not a respectable person
amongst them, but one."

She made a mental reservation in favour of
the large dandy, whom Mrs. Tregarthen felt persuaded she could have taken captive, had she
been a very few years younger, and unmarried,
of course!

"It was a pleasant house, too, they kept,"
said the rector, with a kindly remembrance of
that '64 claret.

"Pleasant house!" repeated his wife. "Pleasant enough, no doubt, and I daresay they kept
pleasant houses in the Cities of the Plain. Such
waste! Such extravagance! Such vanity and
vexation of spirit! I'm sure I did not feel like
a Christian woman till I'd got through the lodge
gate again, going home. When I was told
next day they had brought the poor young man

back on a stretcher, I wasn't the least bit surprised!"

"Did you learn how Mrs."—(somehow the name stuck in his throat)—"how the widow was left?" asked Strange, with kindly interest and practical good sense.

"Badly enough, I fancy, but that won't make much matter to her, from all I hear. Of course I say nothing; it's not my way to interest myself in the affairs of other people, and I haven't a particle of curiosity—never had from a girl. But I *should* like to know who pays for everything now; whether it's that high and mighty Lord there used to be such stories about, who seemed to think his society too good for the world in general, or some of those gay young officers in the Guards, or the handsome man that talked to you, Silas, about Stonehenge. I shouldn't wonder if she got something out of them all!"

There are noble natures, besides that of the

horse, inclined to press against a stab that probes
them to the quick.

" Where is she now? " asked Strange, and
his voice sounded so harsh, that Mrs. Tregarthen
looked sharply in his face, over the rim of her
tumbler, while she drained it to the dregs.

" London," was her answer, "and in London
she is likely to remain. If you ask me, I should
say it suited her to perfection. In a country
place, or even such a town as this, her goings-on
could not pass unnoticed; but in London people
seem to do as they like, and will, I suppose, till
it rains down fire and brimstone from heaven."

The rector's wife, whose familiarity with the
Scriptures placed much powerful imagery at her
command, mentioned such a phenomenon as she
might an ordinary shower, while she put on her
goloshes and prepared to depart. The return
train was punctual to time, and she had various
packages to collect on her way to the station.

" You'll come over and see us at Combe-

Appleton," she said, cordially enough, while shaking hands with Strange, who attended her to the fly, walking like a man in a dream.—"No, my good woman, certainly not!" she added in the same breath, shaking her head at a pale, travel-worn, miserable looking creature, who had not asked for anything, though obviously so weak she could hardly stand. "It's my belief you're tipsy now—as tipsy as you can be, and if I see a policeman I'll tell him to take you in charge."

Then she gathered up her wraps, hurried her husband, and drove off with a good conscience in her breast, a good luncheon somewhat lower down, and a conviction that she was a good Samaritan, who had done a good day's work in a good cause.

The poor, fainting, fasting woman looked after the well-dressed, well-fed lady, as she pulled up the fly window, with a wistful, half-reproachful air, more as it seemed in sorrow than in anger.

"Drunk!" she repeated; "God forgive you,

as I do! Not a bite nor sup has passed my lips
since yesterday morning at daybreak. I haven't
a penny in my pocket, nor a roof to my head,
nor scarce a petticoat to cover me; and when
you're tucked up in bed to-night I'll likely lie
down on these cold stones to die!"

Mrs. Tregarthen, calling at her ironmongers'
for a warming-pan under repair, was far out of
earshot; but Mervyn Strange overheard the
poor thing's mutterings, and partly gathered
their import. Something in the woman's air
and figure stirred his heart to an interest stronger
than mere compassion, though it is but justice
to say that had she been an Albino instead of un-
mistakably a gipsy, he would have turned aside to
afford her relief. He never forgot the example
of his Master, amongst whose manifold perfec-
tions there is but one that humanity can imitate,
at an immeasurable distance, indeed, but with
humble reliance on Him for assistance,—the pri-
vilege of doing good. Where a man goes out

of his way to pick up the fallen, feed the hungry, or console the miserable, he is, for the time being, a true disciple and loyal follower of his Lord.

"You're ill, I am afraid, my good woman," said the clergyman in a kind voice, contrasting pleasantly with the chidings of Mrs. Tregarthen. "What is it? I am afraid there is something more than hunger the matter here."

She lifted her large dark eyes to his—how they reminded him of somebody!—and smiled feebly, while she tried to curtsey her thanks.

"I'm fasting, sir," said she; "but I doesn't feel the hunger and thirst so much. It's the chills I've got, and a pain here, all about my heart; and that's what makes me so bad."

And she leaned against the porch of the "Bull and Boot-jack," shaking like a leaf. In experience with his sick poor he had acquired enough medical knowledge to assure him the woman was very ill, and ought to be put to bed without delay. He had organized, since he came to Boarshaven, nobody knows at what expenditure of time, pains, and energy, a haphazard kind of hospital, into which those were taken whose only claim was that they had none elsewhere; and to this refuge he at once conducted her, leaning on his arm, through the one principal street of the town with as matter-of-course an air as if a ragged gipsy were the fittest companion for a professional-looking divine in a long frock-coat. The inhabitants stared after him with a qualified approval that denoted there was nothing new in such vagaries.

"It's on'y payson wi' some tinker's trull," said a most unkempt dame, who seemed to persuade herself she was cleaning her house by pouring dirty water along the floor. "He've a good heart, have payson. I do know it, and so do *you!*"

"He be *a man*, be payson!" replied the gentleman addressed, an amphibious person, chewing tobacco. "A man, I'se warn! take 'un how you will."

In the course of their progress his charge
afforded Strange such information as she thought
proper on her previous history and present pro-
spects.

"She was a gipsy," she said, "and her name
was Nance—Nance Lovel, that was her right
name, and the name of her people. A gipsy
born and bred, and never knew what it was to
want till she married out of her kin. Yes,
married a Cooper—Zachary Cooper. He wasn't
a Romany, though, nor yet half a Romany, for
all his gipsy name, and—there! she wished she
had cut her right hand off first; but it was no
use talking about that. Well, they had come
west looking for work. Times was very bad, particularly in Zachary's trade. He were a tinker
by rights, but he could turn his hand to almost
any odd job. He liked drinking, though, more
was the pity, a precious sight better than work.
He was at it now ten miles back on the road.
She had been forced to come on by herself, for

she was starving—it was God's truth—starving ;
but she could have made shift too if it hadn't
been for the shivers and the pain that took her
just before his honour came by. There it was
again ! She begged his honour's pardon, she
couldn't hardly bear it when it came on so sharp
and keen."

But they had reached their haven at last,
and poor Nance was turned over to a dear,
matronly, cheerful-looking woman, who treated
all patients alike with the calm forbearance of in-
disputable superiority, from the maimed soldier
six feet high, to the child in arms sickening with
measles or whooping-cough.

Walking home to the dinner that must long
since have got cold, Mervyn Strange was conscious, with mingled feelings of pleasure and
pain dashed by some self-contempt, that he had
by no means forgotten Beltenebrosa so completely as he hoped. The very mention of her
name by Mrs. Tregarthen had stirred his heart

to the core. That lady's account of his lost love, and charitable deductions from her manner of life, had pierced him to the quick. It taxed all his self-command to assume such a composure as might prevent even the rector, by no means an observant person, from detecting his weakness; but he despaired of having concealed it from that lynx in petticoats, the rector's wife. Just now, too, taking this poor suffering tramp to the hospital, every turn of her gipsy figure, every glance of her gipsy eyes, went through him like a knife, recalling the looks, and bearing, and gestures of the girl he had loved so wildly and so well.

"There are no demoniacs in these days," he said to himself, with the irresistible tendency of the human mind to refer anything to the supernatural that passes the bounds of its own limited comprehension, "and our Church gives us small encouragement to believe in the actual bodily presence of the powers of darkness; yet it *does* seem as if an evil spirit had been permitted to take the form of an angel that it might persecute *me*, vile, unworthy, yet most unwilling to sin against knowledge, with its haunting, engrossing, too delightful presence. Why can I not drive this woman from my memory as I have driven her out of my heart? Why must I think of her, dream of her, care for her still, when I know and am resolved that I shall never look on her face again?"

CHAPTER XLIX.

A GREAT GULF.

At his own door, on his very threshold, calm and beautiful as the angel who warned our first parents from the gates of Paradise, yet with something of expectation and humility that he had never seen before in her dear face, stood Beltenebrosa, pale and tall, in a black dress, neither demon nor spectre, but the unforgotten woman who caused all the sorrow he had yet known in life!

Was he awake or dreaming? With a strong effort he pulled himself together, as it were, and stood on his defence.

"Mr. Strange," said the well-known voice, low, impressive, and deliberate, as of old, "you are surprised to see me here—you are surprised to see me at all! Well you may be! Shall I tell you why I have come?"

What did he expect? That she should fall on his breast and declare her love at his feet and implore her forgiveness? Entreat him for shelter? Reproach him for indifference? Excuse herself for desertion? Nothing seemed improbable and extravagant, compared with her appearance here at his very door; and as no language could have conveyed his astonishment, he fell back on the most conventional of all greetings in common use.

"How do you do, Miss Lee?" said he,—"I beg your pardon, Mrs. Paravant. Won't you—won't you come in out of the cold?"

She complied, marching into the house before him, with the haughty grace he remembered only too fondly, marking, we may be sure, every detail of his home—the plain furniture, the littered writing-table, the unadorned chimneypiece, no flowers, no china, no looking-glass, not even a bundle of paper-lights, nor a photograph-book under lock and key.

It mattered little to *her*, she thought, though with a sigh of relief; but obviously in celibacy he still possessed his soul, and there was no Mrs. Strange! If she saw his agitation, and approved, she forbore to notice it, but stood upright, resting her hand on the back of a chair in a queenish attitude of command, somewhat out of character with the part she came to play. In his preoccupation he neither took one himself nor offered her a seat. When people are nerved for a struggle, they keep on their legs as long as they can.

"Mr. Strange," she began, in her fine measured accents, "I have come to you not for assistance, nor even sympathy, but for counsel. I do not beg for it as a favour; you are a minister of the Gospel, and I demand it as a right."

To his honour be it said, the *man* was lost in the *profession*, even while she spoke. No physician who heals the body could have more promptly sank his own identity in the consideration of *a case,* than did this follower of the Physician of souls divest himself of all earthly interests and longings, in his eagerness to fulfil the duties of his calling.

His dignity reasserted itself, his bearing became assured, his voice firm, while he answered,

"Certainly, as *a right.* It is my duty to hear and help and advise as best I may."

"I am very unhappy," she continued. "I need scarcely go into my past history to tell you why. My flight from the rectory was a mistake, my self-dependence was a mistake, my marriage was a mistake,—my whole life has been a mistake. I know it now, when it is too late!"

If there was something pleasing to the man in this comprehensive confession of failure, no symptom of satisfaction betrayed itself on the countenance of the priest, while he remonstrated gravely.

"It is *never* too late," said he, "for repentance and reparation. Were you thrice your age I should remind you of those who came even at the eleventh hour. But for *you*, with the promise of a lifetime before you, how can it be too late to repent and reform, and leave the broad road for the narrow way?"

Was he thinking of Mrs. Tregarthen's malicious stories and insinuations, or did a sense of clemency for the sinner make him unusually severe upon the sin?

"Am I then so *very* bad?" she asked meekly enough. "Useless, selfish, and frivolous I know, but surely not so wicked as you seem to think!"

"I am not your judge," he answered sternly. "I can admonish, and I can reprove; but I can no more *convince* you of your offences than I can pardon them."

"You will believe me, at any rate," she continued, impatiently, and with feminine inconsequence, "when I tell you that I am very unhappy, and tired of everything. I have tried gaiety, I have tried adventure : the first wearied, the second disappointed me. One day seems so exactly like another. I want to lead a different life. I want to be good."

"For a change?" he asked, with some severity.

"For a change! Why not? A change for the better, surely, in such a case as mine. I have come down here to this out-of-the-way corner of the world that I might break off old associations, get rid of old habits, and begin a new life, a life of usefulness and self-denial, with nothing to hinder and drag me back."

"You have counted the cost? You mean what you say?"

"Do you not know me yet? When did I ever say more or less than I meant? Will you help me?"

He pondered. She seemed in earnest; and it was not for *him*, least of all in his priestly capacity, to balk her in these meritorious designs. In his experience, even at Boarshaven, he had known more than one such penitent, fascinated, so to speak, by the picturesque side of a religion that testifies itself in good works, who had fallen away sadly before the realities of the task when it was found to impose many unpleasant and irk-some details. Nevertheless, she demanded a trial, and she must have it.

"You want to begin at once?" he said, marking the subdued impatience on that face he knew so well.

"To-day, if I can," she answered. "I will go amongst your poor, visit them, read to them, succour them; teach the children, comfort the afflicted, and look after the sick."

The practical part of his mind reverted instantly to his hospital.

"Have you had any experience in such matters?" he asked. "An ignorant nurse is worse than none."

"I was with poor James till he died," she answered, with tears in her eyes. "The doctor said I took to nursing as readily as if I had served my time in a hospital. Poor James! Constant care could not save him, or he would have been alive now."

"I will not dissuade you," said the clergyman, with increased reserve. "If you really repent of a misspent life and wasted opportunities, I approve of your resolution. If you are unhappy, there is no remedy for sorrow like constant occupation in the effort to do good. I know it by myself," he added, ruefully, "for I too have fallen, and suffered, and repented, and, I hope, been forgiven."

The sadness of his tone cut her to the heart. He seemed so changed, so exalted, so completely removed from her world, like some disembodied spirit purified by death. And it was her own doing! This man, now so utterly lost to her, might once have been—nay, *was*—her slave, and

she threw him aside without a scruple. How
could she? How could she? After such an outrage as she had inflicted, he would never come
back again : to that she must reconcile herself as
best she might. Was it because he seemed to
repudiate her utterly that she felt she loved him
dearly, and could not live without him? Yes,
this was part of a punishment already greater
than she could bear.

He was very practical when they came to
practical things. Had she a respectable lodging
—was it in a healthy part of the town? Boarshaven could not boast of the best sanitary arrangements, and had hardly been drained at all. He
hoped to do something in time to remedy even
these material defects. The fact was, you got at
the moral being of people through their physical
wants. His hospital, he hoped, had done as
much good to souls as bodies. Would she like to
begin helping him in this hospital to-morrow?—
to-day? Then she was *really* in earnest! Well,

he had taken a poor woman there (he was going
to say a *gipsy*-woman, but checked himself) not
an hour ago. Sickening, he feared, of fever.
Perhaps it would be too great a risk. If she
insisted, he would go with her himself. Afterwards, he had a Mechanics' Institute to lecture,
and his night-school to attend, and, in fact, every
minute of his time was engaged for the rest of
the evening.

So they parted — very unlike lovers, she
thought bitterly—with no kind of understanding,
expressed or inferred, that they were to meet
again; and Beltenebrosa felt the tears rise warm
to her eyes, while she wondered if it was to be
so the next day, and the day after, and all the
rest of their lives.

They seemed far more apart now than even
on that fatal occasion when they met so un-
expectedly in Boarshaven parish church, that she
might leave it James Paravant's bride.

And the curate went his way, to work hard

in his obscure corner of the vineyard, breaking the clods with that dogged persistency which never fails to succeed at last, and walked home in the dark, thoroughly tired-out, and went to bed, and dreamed a dream.

He thought he was on a wide level plain with here and there a bush, and here and there a tree —all looming hazy and indistinct in the vapoury mist that sometimes comes at moonrise. He felt impelled, with the usual inconsistency of such visions, to glide on smooth and swift, like one who skates rather than walks, for no obvious reason, and in no defined course; but when he tried to stop, his feet seemed to bear him forward against his will. The grass grew high in places—waist-high, he believed—but he could not tell, for he skimmed along its top, which neither bent nor rustled beneath his tread. A star shone faintly through the mist that thickened every moment. He felt glad of its glimmer to direct his steps, though he knew and did not care that his wanderings were without end or aim, and all directions were alike.

Suddenly, but without shock or effort, he stopped short, and found himself on the brink of a running stream, too wide to leap, too deep to wade, too swift to stem or swim. His brain turned like a wheel as he fixed his eyes on the farther bank, across the rushing waters that careered between.

On that bank stood a phantom, waving, gesticulating in piteous mute appeal, imploring him to come. Its form was vague and unsubstantial, its garb, its shape, its very lineaments were dissolved in the mist; but through that floating vapour shone two large, loving, beseeching eyes, and they were the eyes of Beltenebrosa, formerly Jane Lee.

He scanned the stream that parted them, and took in its perils at a glance. No spring could cover it from bank to bank; no swimmer could make head for two strokes against that pouring torrent. The attempt must be death. But the mist grew thicker every moment; the phantom beckoned "Come!" He set his teeth, he held his breath, he braced his muscles for a leap, he put his hands together for a header,——awoke in the effort, and behold, it was a dream!

CHAPTER L.

THE FAITHFUL SERVANT.

THIS hard-working curate, so well known to the vilest of the vile in the dirty alleys of Boarshaven, was a very different character from the Mervyn Strange of old undergraduate days, or even the assistant of an easy-going rector in a quiet parish of West Somerset. Like all men who fill a useful part in the world, he had so enlarged his views that they scarcely seemed to comprise the same objects now, and had got rid of enough prejudices to set up half a dozen young beginners in his trade. At five-and-twenty he was a priest, at five-and-thirty a parson. The

L 2

distinction was of his own drawing, and he explained thus :

As in the different periods of historical warfare, he argued, different tactics and a different class of soldiers have been found necessary, so is it with that noblest of all campaigns, the struggle of good against evil, the conduct of which is entrusted to the Church Militant on earth. You wanted formerly a knight in armour, impervious to the weak and clumsy projectiles of his time, as you wanted a priest in his vestments, whose sacred pomp and presumptive infallibility should impose on the vulgar minds, untaught to reason, assailable only by the outward senses of eye and ear. The knight in mail and plate rode down unarmed men in battle; the priest with his awful weapons of excommunication and absolution set aside the stoutest opposition to his will with a Latin sentence and a wave of his hand: gunpowder and printing have destroyed the supremacy of both. Now that the general rate of intelligence has so increased, and the man who can neither read nor write is the exception rather than the rule, our contests, moral or physical, must be waged on corresponding principles; we must attack in a looser formation, with more self-reliance, and at the same time more mutual support; above all, more versatility to meet the constant changes of front and increased activity of the foe. The soldier, in these days, must be a man of science, a man of business, and even a man of the world; the clergyman, too, requires, on the same principle, and perhaps not in a less degree than during the troubled times of the primitive Church, that wisdom of the serpent, which is no unbecoming adjunct to the innocence of the dove.

"I can do more good," said Strange, "as the parson than the priest;" and he threw aside, not without a pang, many of those ornamental vanities of his profession, which are as dear to the Cloth as his horse-furniture and trappings to the

Hussar. Though he dressed in sober black, and still wore the flowing frock-coat, chiefly, I believe, because he could not afford a new one, he laid aside all those dandyisms of white cambric and black silk in which his youth had delighted. He intoned no longer through his nose, in sing-song, from the reading-desk, nor mumbled below his breath at the altar. In his sermons, he insisted less on the supremacy of a Church than the brotherhood of a community, addressing his congregation with the friendly remonstrances of a transgressor like themselves, who prayed, and hoped, and tried to do better, rather than frightening weaker and irritating stronger minds by insisting on an impossible standard it seemed hopeless to attain, and of which no very tempting example was afforded, in violent invective and denunciations of unreasonable wrath.

He was of opinion, too, that he could do more good by visiting his parishioners in their homes, than by reading three sermons a day to his clerk and the pew-women; nor did he consider an incessant ringing of bells indispensable to the doctrine, discipline, and prosperity of a Christian Church.

I am not quite sure that the women thoroughly liked his discourses : to such arguments as assailed their reason they did not listen, and listening, would not have understood; while in his eloquent appeals to their feelings they sadly missed those reiterated assurances of eternal misery for the great bulk of mankind, that seem to the gentler sex a comfort and satisfaction it is difficult to comprehend.

But for the honest, hard-handed bread-winners, the heads of families, who toiled heartily all the week, but were prone to fall into the snares of Satan and John Barleycorn on Saturday night, " Payson," as they called him, was really a guide, philosopher, and friend. He never withheld manly rebuke; he told them to their faces that they were fools to squander a day's earnings on an hour's debauch, and beasts to indulge in excess when the children wanted shoes; but he never ignored the strength of their temptations, nor refused that sympathy to such as had given way, without which human nature turns dogged and morose, sinking from bad to worse, till it becomes insensible alike to kindness and reproof.

The women also, when they came to know how courageous a temperament accompanied his unfailing kindness of heart, approved of him mightily, as seen in their own homes. They appreciated that courtesy to their sex which is the unerring mark of a gentleman, and flopped their dirty dusters over their dirty chairs with all the more cordiality of welcome that he removed his hat, the instant he crossed the lowliest threshold, as scrupulously as if he were entering the drawing-room of a duchess.

They wondered at him for the first few months, the tradespeople especially, many of whom, resenting his scanty means and narrow

expenditure, insinuated that he was a humbug;
but by the time his night-school had filled and
his hospital was fairly started, all ranks were
constrained to admit in their own extraordinary
vernacular that "Payson, he do be a good sort—
uncommon!" And though he never expected it,
even here, in the squalid alleys of Boarshaven,
inhabited by the most untidy population in
England, he did not miss his reward.

It is on such men as these that some angel,
taking an interest in the episcopacy, pounces now
and then to make a bishop. Who can tell
whether they do as much good in the wider as
the narrower sphere? At any rate, they serve
where they are ordered, and some day, when the
secrets of all hearts are made known, who can
doubt they will hear in heaven those gracious
words of approval their whole lives on earth
have been spent to win?

Our sailors, according to Dibdin, cherish a
pleasing fancy that

"There's a sweet little cherub who sits up aloft,
To take care of the life of poor Jack."

And it would be well if some shipmate of this friendly little guardian were told off for the same humane duty, as regards a poor parson's heart.

We have never been taught that St. Anthony, though he must have sadly required it, received any visible assistance from above; and as the ideal of woman, to many temperaments, is even more formidable than her reality, he must have had a roughish time when beautiful shapes, arrayed rather than dressed for conquest, were flitting round him in swarms. The little cherub might have rendered no small aid to the saint; might render no small aid now to many a bachelor parson through the length and breadth of England, whose heart, large in every other sense, is small, like his income, in this, that it can only find room for one woman at a time.

Now that lawn-tennis has displaced croquet, and become the engrossing occupation of both sexes under five-and-thirty, at all hours of the day, how is he to escape?

Every garden and pleasure-ground in his own and other parishes is filled with *Houris*,—black-eyed, blue-eyed, grey-eyed (the last very dangerous), proffering claret-cup instead of sherbet, and waving their scarfs, green or otherwise, to the true believer, if only they can persuade him to believe in *them!* Eyes, cheeks, and lips glow with exercise and health; shapely forms take every imaginable attitude of grace and freedom, in the exigencies of the game. Sweet voices laugh and coo and murmur. "*Won't* you be my partner?" says one. "You and I can do it easily," whispers another. "I'm *so* afraid of *you* for an adversary," smiles a third; and the undefended captive feels he could not be more helpless were he involved bodily in the meshes of that insidious net, stretched between his enslavers and himself, in a mere mockery of prohibition. Yes, next to a picnic, especially in wet weather, which may be termed a "certainty," I think a garden party to play lawn-tennis is, of all the fields in which man meets his fair enemy so clumsily, the most likely to ensure his discomforture and defeat.

Now, there were young ladies even at Boarshaven; there were lawns and gardens within easy distance of the town; need I say there were rackets, balls, chalked-out courts, and lovely players, ready to take every advantage of the game? Yet in less than six months one and all had given up Mervyn Strange for a bad job. The man seemed adamant. He was stiff, they told one another (that was when each had given him up for everybody else); he was pompous; he was a bear! Papa liked to have him, because he thought him so useful in the parish, but even when papa invited him one couldn't get him to come. He was odd, certainly. Good-looking? Oh, *dear* no! What about age? Oh, a hundred! Why, the man's hair was quite grey. They had asked him to dinner, wanting to be civil, which wasn't absolutely necessary, for, after all, you know, they never asked the other curate ; but he refused, and even mamma said it was no use.

Presently they left off chasing him, wistful and ashamed, one after another, like a pack of fox-hounds that have been running hare, and the opinion of every young lady within the Boarshaven circuit of that walking postman who so deplored Valentine's Day was that Mr. Strange might be honest, well-meaning, intellectual, and a painstaking clergyman ; but, individually, one could not quite like him, because he had no heart !

How little they knew ! And that heart, which they voted he did *not* possess, had been aching for months in a loneliness that he now looked back to as comparative comfort and repose. He was sad then, and dull enough in spirits, but at least he had the approval of his own conscience, and a sense of self-reliance that waits on steady

perseverance in the path of rectitude and common sense. Now he was haunted! Yes, haunted
—no other word could express the delusion
under which he laboured, the spell against which
he fought. Not in vain! No; he was resolved
it should not be in vain. As a man puts from
him the promptings of an evil spirit, or resists in
some hideous dream the invitations of a fiend,
so would he strive against the influence this
woman had come here to regain, and resolve, if
necessary, though they should live in the same
town, nay, in the same street, never to set eyes
on her fatal beauty again.

"Could you not have left me in peace?" he
groaned, waking up from those dreams, sleeping
or waking, that always recalled the same pale,
proud, handsome face. "What had I done to you
that you should persecute and torment me for
ever? You have robbed me of all my happiness
in this world. Take it and welcome; but you
shall not rob me of all my hope for the next!"

CHAPTER LI.

GOOD WORKS.

BELTENEBROSA, I need hardly observe at this stage of my narrative, was not a person who did things by halves. In less than a week she settled herself as the occupant of a decent first floor in the cleanest house she could find, to the intense bewilderment of a landlady who had never seen anything to compare with this lodger before, and talked about her from morning to night. She organized a regular routine of duties amongst the poor, especially those who were sick, and took stated hours of attendance at the hospital, where the Matron, who at first sadly mistrusted her fine appearance and white hands, declared she was as good as any two paid nurses for "helpfulness," as she called it, and had better nerve than most surgeons. She was never tired of enlarging on the merits of her paragon to Mervyn Strange, who listened with unbroken patience, though usually inclined to cut her volubility rather short, for this energetic functionary, like many other trustworthy and invaluable women, loved to hear the music of her own tongue. It seemed unaccountable, however, and even uncourteous, that he studiously avoided visiting his favourite institution at the same hours as Mrs. Paravant.

"I'd like you to see her," said the Matron, delighted to get a listener, "walking through my wards and passages, smooth and noiseless as a shadow. If they're asleep, not one of them wakes when she passes by. If they're hot and restless, tossing and turning, poor things, she don't go to aggravate them, mincing, and sidling, and whispering : worse than if you were to beat a drum in their ears, as I know well, being used to sick people and their ways. Her very clothes, though they look so fresh and new, don't seem to rasp and rustle not half as bad as my own; and many's the time, if you'll believe me, Mr. Strange, I damp a clean petticoat to take the starch out, till it's as limp as a rag."

"You consider her an efficient nurse?" asked the clergyman, waiving further details of the good lady's toilet.

"It's no word for her," was the enthusiastic answer. "If nurses came straight down from heaven, she could hold her own with the best. I needn't remind *you*, Mr. Strange—a clergyman, and a *good* clergyman too—of what comes out of the mouth of babes and suchlike, after they're weaned, of course. Our little Jem Vialls—that mite of a thing in Number Two, with his poor little thigh broke, you know;—well, I looked in to see if he was asleep, yesterday about this time, and I found the dear laughing to his little self, as pleased as Punch. 'What is it, Jem?' says I; 'leg doesn't hurt so bad now?' says I. 'Oh, mother,' says Jem—he always calls me mother, poor innocent, having none of his own —'what do you think?' says he; 'I was dreaming of the angels in heaven, and I woke up so quick, there was one of them left that hadn't time to fly away. She tucked me up, and kissed me, and she's to come again every day till I get well. Do you suppose, mother,' says he, 'she'll take me with her when she goes back for good?' Then I knew, as if I'd seen her, that Mrs. Paravant had been nursing the boy; and if she's not exactly an angel now, she will have wings of her own some day, or I'm very much mistaken."

How could he listen to such trash? He was ten minutes behindhand already, yet he lingered curiously, loth to go.

"That fever case?" he asked,—"the gipsy who came in last week. Is there any hope she will recover?"

" There's *every* hope ! " answered the Matron. " But here again, Mr. Strange, I tell you fair, it's not the doctor that has pulled her through, but the nurse. He says so himself. He told Mrs. Paravant the same. ' I'm only the medicine,' says he, with his old-fashioned bow. ' You, ma'am, are the food and the fresh air, and the blessed sunshine into the bargain. I showed the patient the way upstairs, I admit, but it's *you*, ma'am, *you*, who took her under the arms, and hoisted her, step by step, to the first landing. I congratulate you, ma'am,' says he, ' and some day you'll get your reward.' I never saw our doctor take so much snuff, Mr. Strange, since I've known him ; that showed he meant all he said ! ' Ah ! you give me a hundred such nurses as Mrs. Paravant, and I'll undertake to clear every hospital this side Severn by next Easter-Day ! ' But you can't find 'em, Mr. Strange, you can't find 'em, and that's the truth ! "

He was the last man to dispute it. Must it be always so? Was it not enough that she should haunt his thoughts and his dreams? Must he also hear her praises on every tongue? find witnesses to her merits at every turn? It was a hard battle, much harder than he expected. His weaker nature longed to lay down its arms, ask for quarter, and confess itself beat; but that weaker nature, kept under control from boyhood, should not dictate to him now.

" Will you walk through the fever ward, sir?" asked the Matron, with that sudden relapse into official gravity common to her class, as to wardens, inspectors of police, and non-commissioned officers in the army. " It's a chance if we don't find Mrs. Paravant there now. I *should* like for you to see her at work; she's so quiet, and helpful, and earnest. Grave and thoughtful too. Just like yourself, sir. I often think she's not quite easy in her mind; but I wouldn't take the liberty of asking her. I

dursn't, Mr. Strange, to tell the truth, and that's
a good deal for me to confess."

No; he wouldn't visit the fever ward just
then; he was pressed for time. He would come
back later when there was nobody to disturb
the patient, if she would like him to read to
her. The last time she seemed too unwell to
listen.

The Matron smiled. "We can't undertake
to cure her so far as *that*, sir," she answered.
"You may read the Bible to these gipsies till
you're hoarse, and never a word will they understand from end to end, and wouldn't if they
could. It's bred in them, Mr. Strange; they
can't help it. Vagabond, heathen, savage is the
gipsy from birth. Like the wolves, if you take
them home and tame them, they're as wild and
fierce as ever again the day they get loose.
Bodies they have tough as pin-wire, and con-
stitutions splendid! It's a pleasure to nurse
them; but as for souls! in my opinion, Mr.

Strange, they haven't got any, though I beg your pardon, sir—you know best."

Neglecting to set her right on a question in which she must be so egregiously mistaken, the curate departed without further parley, and Beltenebrosa, who knew his step amongst a thousand, felt her heart tighten and the tears come to her eyes, that he should thus avoid her with deliberate and heartless coldness, here in the fever ward of his hospital as in the streets of the town or the few mild social gatherings in which there seemed the slightest chance they would meet.

It was impossible for a woman like Mrs. Paravant to remain unnoticed even in so quiet a place as Boarshaven. Mervyn Strange was not the only clergyman in the place, and the routine of her self-imposed duties brought her in contact with the other curate, an honest young fellow, who admired beauty and loved cricket; also with the rector, a grave divine nearly superan-

nuated. Both these churchmen, though they
thought him a little mad, highly esteemed their
coadjutor, and were willing to receive with cordial civility this wonderful nurse of his importa-
tion. The elder, indeed, thought it would be as
well if she were not quite so good-looking; but
the younger seemed of a different opinion.
Both, however, expressed and showed a desire to
make her stay amongst them as agreeable as
they could. The rector's wife also, too advanced
in years to be prejudiced against the beauty she
professed to admire, pronounced at once that
this dark handsome person was a lady born.
She knew the stamp, she hoped, and could not
be mistaken, for her mamma's own brother was
a baronet (*Vide* Burke's "Titles Extinct"), and
she had herself been presented at Court.

So Mrs. Paravant was asked to a quiet afternoon tea, and came; and being put through her
facings, was made to confess she was a Paravant
of Combe-Wester, to find herself vastly increased

in importance by the admission, as belonging to
one of the county families of a neighbouring
shire. In her own short apprenticeship, while
she kept house for "forward James," she had
been obliged to study that inexplicable table of
precedence for which there are no written rules;
and acknowledged, though she could not understand, the superiority a marsh on Severn-side
conferred over a block of houses in Boarshaven
town. The rector's wife exulted. "There was
no mistaking the old blood," she said, "nor
deceiving those who possessed it. She knew the
woman for a lady at a glance."

And Beltenebrosa lingered over her luke-
warm tea, and watched and waited, glancing at
the door, and he never came.

It was the same thing day after day. That
desire which feeds on disappointment, is of all
the most engrossing, the most demoralizing, and
the hardest to subdue. Sometimes she caught
sight of his well-known figure hurrying round a

corner, and felt her heart sink with the consciousness that it vanished purposely on her approach.
Sometimes, meeting him in his rounds, he would
turn deliberately before they were face to face,
and walk away in an opposite direction. Once
they came into collision—there was no other word
for it—in a dark and squalid hovel, where an old
crone lay dying: he spoke firmly and coldly,
without the slightest symptom of emotion, on the
necessities of the case; and she answered in the
same tone. Would all her senses have thrilled
with rapture to know that under this unflinching
assumption of self-command, his heart was beating more wildly and aching more cruelly than
her own?

In her vexation and despair she sometimes
thought of that last resource by which a woman
tries to recover a lost empire at the sacrifice, often
fruitless, of her own dignity and self-respect.

"Shall I make him jealous?" said she, and
despised herself for the suggestion. There was

plenty of material to her hand : the other curate, an aspiring solicitor given to good works, two or three young gentlemen learning to raise rents and shoot wild partridges, at a neighbouring land agent's, one and all would have waited no second hint to fall at her feet; but something in the pride of her wild nature, some innate sense of fidelity to *herself*, rather than another, forbade the degradation, and she let them sigh in vain. Beltenebrosa was "going through the mile," so to speak—was being subjected to that course of training which strengthens, purifies, and exalts the moral being, even as discipline and sudorifics dissolve humours in the physical frame. She had the good sense to know it, telling herself, in all humility, that she was suffering for past unworthiness, and it was only right that one whose life had formerly centred solely in self should be punished by the *peine forte et dure* of discovering that her whole existence was merged in another.

Some dispositions, under continued disappointment, sink into apathy and despair; not so
with hers : no woman with those mobile features
and flashing eyes could shrug her shoulders, fold
her hands, and say "What's the use?" Evil or
good, she must be doing. It seemed fortunate
that at such a juncture the good lay nearer to
her hand than the evil, and, what is of more importance, nearer also to her heart. In walking
these long rounds, the very physical exercise was
beneficial; and who can dwell entirely on mental
sufferings, however acute, in presence of bodily
agony crying out for relief? That she was tread-
ing in the curate's very steps, that she passed
through the doors he had lately closed, hung
over the bed at which even now he stood, beautiful in the brightness of those who bring good
tidings; that she shared his dangers, as his toils;
tending the same contagious disorders, breathing
the same fever-laden air; that she might come
across him by accident at any moment, on the

field where they both fought so gallantly; all this she tried hard not to consider, forcing herself to accept the situation for its own sake, whatever might be the result. Here was the lesson of humility she must learn. Here was the task of reparation she must fulfil. She would go through with it to the end.

CHAPTER LII.

BORN A LOVEL.

To USE an expression of the Matron more forcible than elegant, poor Nance " had a squeak for it." Low fever, fastening on a frame wasted by hard living and hard usage, found little to oppose its ravages, save the innate strength of constitution, that seems the birthright of a people who live and die in the open air. To the spare habit and vigorous temperament of her nation, combined with the patient nursing of Beltenebrosa, Nance owed a recovery that for a time seemed hopeless; for she remained some days insensible, regaining consciousness at the stated period that

Nature seems to have established as her land-mark, a point where the doctor is satisfied he has saved the patient and worsted the disease. When, after a long unbroken sleep succeeding many hours of delirium, Nance opened her black eyes, they expressed in their first glance the cunning and caution of her race. Beltenebrosa knew she was recognized, even before the poor thin hand on the counterpane clung round her own, and raised it to the pale wasted face with a touching gesture of gratitude and devotion.

" Is it *you* that's been nursin' of me, sister?" said Nance, in the trembling accents of exhaus-tion, "or am I dreaming still? If so be I am a-dreaming, don't ye wake me, for pity's sake! Let me go off comfortable; I'll never feel so easy again."

" It *is* Jane Lee," answered the other. "The same Jane Lee you waited on in the Patron's caravan. You're not going to die, Nance; never fear. Keep quiet now; go to sleep again. I

won't leave you; I'll be at your bedside when
you wake."

She had anticipated this untoward recogni-
tion by her gipsy kinswoman, and prepared herself
for all its hazards and inconveniences ; yet were
these none the more acceptable when they came.
She dreaded the discovery of her refuge by
Jericho, his exactions, his audacious advances,
his reckless cupidity, and—and—what would
Mervyn Strange think of her intimacy with such
people as these ?

She need not have distressed herself. Gratitude is one of the few good qualities that the
ban of society has not succeeded in eradicating
from the gipsy's character. Nance felt and
declared she owed her life to the patient assi-
duities of her nurse, and cherished, moreover,
an active sympathy for this stately kinswoman,
who, like herself, had married out of her race.

In the long hours of convalescence she would
dwell, with no little interest, on their similarity

of fortune, envying, I am inclined to think, the good luck of the other in losing a Gentile husband she ought never to have won. No princess of old Spain, no Austrian countess with her sixteen quarterings, no Percy, Howard, Seymour, or Somerset of our own nobility could have laid greater store by the transmission of pure blood from generation to generation, than did this gipsy tramp, with her ragged petticoat, shapely figure, slender hands, arched feet, and dirty, high-bred face.

"I can't think how I come to do it, sister," she argued; "and if I wasn't regular bewitched, I'm sure I couldn't have been in my right mind. Born a Lovel, as you know, nothing can't rob me of that; and to take up with one of them Coopers, and him not a *real* Cooper neither! It doesn't seem like sense, and yet it's true—too true, as I feel every day, to my cost!"

"But I suppose you liked him?" observed the nurse, wondering, with some self-scorn, that

she, of all people, should take an interest in a
love story.   Had she not done with such follies
for ever?   Had she not gathered the flowers to
find only poison in their petals?   And could she
hanker after the scent of them still?

"That's just where it is," answered Nance.
" How was I to be off liking of him—so pleasant-
spoken, so obliging?   ' Let *me* fill the pail for
you, my dear,' says he ; ' those beautiful slender
fingers of yourn oughtn't never to know the
touch of hard work.   You'll come to the fair
with *me,* my dark-eyed Nance, and if there's
aught good enough to set off that comely face of
yourn, I'll spend a week's wages but what I'll
have it !'   Now it's ' Blast ye ! why isn't the
kettle a-bilin' for my grog?   There you be, as
usual, washin' of your face and combin' of your
hair, when you ought to be mindin' your work ! '
And as for black eyes, sister, I've an extra pair
as doesn't set off a woman's good looks, oftener
than not, along of his cruel fists.   He've a heavy

hand, have my Zachary, and, though he be but a little chap, bless ye! he's as strong as a bull."

"I should leave him, dear, if I were you," exclaimed Beltenebrosa, firing with womanly indignation at this recital of conjugal wrongs. "I wouldn't live a day with a man who dared to lift his hand against me. Not an hour!"

"It's easy talking," answered Nance, wearily, "but what's a poor woman to do? We can't keep ourselves not anything like decent with the little wage our weak fingers can earn at the needle and suchlike. I doesn't think as I could wire a rabbit, even a young one, not if I was starving! We wants a *man* about us, whether or no. Somehow the fire doesn't seem to burn so bright when there's no master a-lightin' of his pipe at the embers; and it's dreary work to wake up at night under the stars and find yourself all alone. No, sister: mine is bad as can be, I'm not going to deny it, and yet a bad husband is a sight better than none at all."

"But you came here alone," urged Beltenebrosa. "The Matron told me that when you were
brought in by—by—Mr. Strange, the day you
were taken so ill, he found you in the street
without a soul to look after you."

"It's God's truth, my dear," was the answer;
"and God's blessing on that tall grand gentleman who picked me out of the very mud in the
roadway. He's fit to be a prince, he is! *There's*
a man, now, as a woman might be proud and
happy to own! He'd never speak a word but
in kindness; he'd never look at her without a
smile; and he'd lay down his life for her, if need
be, just because he is one of the brave loving
sort as thinks her a finer creature than himself,
when she isn't fit to clean his boots! I seen it
in his eyes!"

She had thought so too, of late, a thousand
times. Did his admirable qualities strike her
more forcibly now that they seemed so obvious
even to this rude uneducated kinswoman, who

N 2

had detected his noble nature with the intuition of her sex? Beltenebrosa did not often blush. Nevertheless she turned aside to the window, and changed the subject.

"What shall you do, Nance," she asked, "when you are obliged to leave us? You know we mustn't keep you after you get well."

Nance pondered. "Go back to Zachary," she said, resolutely: "maybe he misses me by now. My Zachary isn't always at his worst, sister. Sometimes it will be fair weather with him days on end. He was on the drink, you see, when him and me parted; but that wouldn't last more nor a week at most, 'specially as he wasn't over-flush of cash, and he's not one as potmen and suchlikes will trust when they doesn't know him, nor, for that matter, when they does. I wouldn't like him to be calling out 'Nance, Nance!' and nobody answer, just as he's down in one of them fits when the liquor has died out and the trembles begins. If you'd

seen him then, sister, you'd pity him, you
would ! "

" Not so much as I pity *you*," thought the
other; but she marvelled at this tenacity of
affection for an unworthy object under its most
unworthy conditions, speculating on the origin
of such fidelity in one of her own kindred, the
tameless race so strong for good and evil. Could
she herself show this constancy, this devotion,
this unchanging loyalty to the idol, however unworthy, she had enshrined in her heart? Yes!
a thousand times yes !

In the meantime certain expressions, certain
turns of face and gestures in her charge, brought
Jericho forcibly to her memory, and she resolved
to learn all she could of her persecutor's movements, on the principle that forewarned is fore-
armed.

" You shall not go away penniless, Nance,"
said she, " I will see to that; and—and—there
is your kinsman, you know—yours and mine—

Jericho Lee. I suppose he would take care you did not starve."

Weak as she was, Nance sat up in bed, crossed her forefingers, and moved her lips as though she spat over them on the floor.

"My curse on him!" said she, in such a hoarse whisper as betrayed the fervency of her hatred. "My curse on Jericho Lee, his tent and his blanket, his kettle and his cup! By wood and stream, by night and day, walking, lying, standing, sitting, asleep or awake, alive or dead, I ban every bone in his body, every hair on his head, that not an inch of him may go uncursed to the grave! And if ever I forgive him, may all the ill I wish him, and ten times more, come upon *me* instead!

"Listen, sister! I am a gipsy, and I have taken a tinker tramp. I was born a Lovel, and I married out of my kindred and out of my degree. It's bad enough, but I might have been a happy woman only for Jericho. He it was

who encouraged my Zachary to love the drink,
and lent him money, the false-hearted villain!
and made him work it out *choring* and thieving,
till he got him in his hands so, as if Jerry do
but lift a finger, he's bound to do his bidding
like a dog! I've known him boast—I heard
him myself; ah! he didn't think as I'd crept
behind the screen—that he'd as good as got a
rope round my man's neck, and could hang him
at a week's notice whenever he took the fancy.
No, sister, there's good and bad of all sorts, but
nobody will make me believe as that there Devil
the tall gentleman mentioned at this very bed-
side could ever be half so black, or a quarter
so wicked, as Jéricho Lee!"

"And where is he now?" asked the other,
with more anxiety than she would have cared to
admit.

"Where's the wind as blows north to-day,
and south to-morrow, and east or west, just as
it happens, the day after? I can't say where

Jericho *is,* sister. I can tell you where I hope
he's *not,* and that's where I seen him last, barely
two days' walk from this town, on the London
road, drinking with my man, giving of him a
trifle of money and a heap of fair words. I
know'd he was up to mischief by that, 'specially
as he seemed all on the high ropes, jawin' and
smilin', with a tall hat and a broadcloth coat,
dressed out like a lord of the land."

"But, Nance," urged Beltenebrosa, "you
must know, you must have heard him say what
made him leave London? Did he mean to come
on here?"

"I might find out from my Zachary," replied
Nance, who could not but observe the anxiety
of her listener. "As soon as I can get on my
feet I'll travel back the way I came, on the track
as my man is pretty sure to follow up. He'll
maybe tell me if he knows; but there, Jerry's
as deep as a well. Only one thing makes me
think as he may be coming to this very town. I

was by when he swore, black as night, he had
never heard of the place, and didn't believe in
it!"

The inference seemed obvious. Beltenebrosa
fairly shuddered when she reflected on the odious
persistency of this man, to avoid whom she had
fled into the remotest corner of the kingdom.
She could neither baffle nor control him. For a
moment she felt very helpless and forlorn. Then
she bethought her of Fighting Jack, his paternal
affection, the stronger for inebriety, his dogged
fidelity to his own warped notions of right, and
the protection afforded by his influence and
personal daring.

"But how came Jericho to be alone?" she
asked. "Where is the Patron?"

"The tall gentleman must tell you *that*,"
answered Nance, with a sad smile. "He says
he knows. I don't. If the Patron is alive anywheres, it's in some place where he'll have to do
without drink and baccy. Clothes, too; but he

won't miss them so bad. Why, didn't you never hear, sister? The Patron has got a grave in London town, just like some Gorgio gentleman as dies in a four-post bed. I wouldn't say but what there's a stone to it, and print. I hope he lies easy, I'm sure, for he'll never get out no more!"

" Is he dead?" gasped the other.

"Dead enough," answered Nance. "Sudden like, they said. Went under as if he'd been shot. We was in the north, Zachary and me, when the news come. I can't mind what the doctor called it, but Jericho says it was gin."

Beltenebrosa fairly broke down. " God help me!" she exclaimed, bursting into tears, " I haven't a friend in the world!"

CHAPTER LIII.

"NOLENS-VOLENS."

LORD ST. MORITZ, in spite of the policeman's anticipations, was obliged to attend an inquest held on the body of Fighting Jack. His own, indeed, seemed the only material evidence, and the whole affair, transacted in a close ill ventilated apartment, occupied very little time. Emerging with some satisfaction into the fresh air, his Lordship was surprised to feel his elbow touched by a slim, dark fellow with the gipsy colouring, that still, by some association of ideas, brought sweet and bitter memories into his heart.

"Can I have a word with you in private, my

Lord?" said this person, who was none other than Jericho Lee.

His Lordship had never been deficient in courage. Scanning the slender proportions of his questioner, he decided that in the event of a struggle he might hold his own well enough, and with little hesitation followed the other into a by-street, where they could converse without interruption. After proceeding a few paces, the nobleman came to a halt.

"Now, then," he said, abruptly, "what is it? You want money, of course."

"I don't look like it," answered Jerry, glancing down at his own flash attire. "But your Lordship knows what's what as well as most, and I *do* want money, that's the truth. I'm not asking you to *give* it me. My Lord, I can tell you something for a fiver that you would part with a hundred willingly to know."

"Say a crown," replied his Lordship, coolly, suspecting this must be some racing "tout"

with false intelligence about a trial or a break-
down. " Five shillings, and I'll take my chance
of your secret not being worth five farthings."

" You won't say that when you know what
it is," returned Jerry. " Look here, my Lord :
five sovereigns, or even four, money down, and
I'll tell you where to find somebody that's been
as good as lost for weeks past."

Though his heart made a great jump, that
steady face betrayed no kind of emotion.

" Nonsense, my good fellow," said he. " Do
you think your information is better than mine ?
Come, if you're hard up, I'll say a pound ; take
it or leave it."

"I'll have to leave it, my Lord. It's not half
enough. Four quid, here on the nail ; that's the
lowest price."

" Then you can leave it, my man, and walk
on. Here, I'll give you a cigar for nothing, if
you want to smoke."

" Your Lordship is a real gentleman. I *should*

like to oblige you.   Won't your Lordship spring
a trifle ? "

"Not a shilling.   I'm very hard at a bargain."

" Well, have it your own way.   Thank you,
my Lord, and I'll take the cigar too, if you please.
She's at Boarshaven, that's where she is.   I
want the money bad, or you wouldn't have got
the tip so cheap."

It was time enough.   Like many others who
live by their wits rather than their wisdom,
Jericho Lee, notwithstanding the fine clothes on
his back, was almost penniless.   It requires
uninterrupted success in shoplifting, picking
pockets, and such branches of unregistered in-
dustry, to stand the expenses incurred by a
fancy man of the swell mob like handsome
Jericho Lee.   The champagne alone swallowed
by his fair friends, at ten shillings a bottle in
the Haymarket, made a fearful hole in his earnings ; and after he had treated one to gloves,

another to boots, and a third to a new hat, there
was little left for himself. This sovereign, so
opportunely extracted, would pay his expenses
to Boarshaven, whither he resolved to follow his
kinswoman, taking a west country fair on his
way, at which merrymaking he hoped to earn
some addition to his resources, by help of that
useful implement the thimble, that homely vegetable the pea.

It was thus he came in contact with Zachary
and Nance, to the deterioration of the tinker, and
extreme discomfiture of his ill-used spouse.

" Boarshaven !" muttered his Lordship, as he
walked away. " Now, what in the name of everything that's unaccountable can have taken her to
such an out-of-the-way hole as that? The fellow
seemed to know all about it. I wish I had asked
him a few more questions. I believe he is a
relation ; something in his face reminded me of
hers. I wish it had not ! I've never done any good
with her from first to last, and that night after

the play was a sickener. I don't suppose she would speak to me now, if we met again. I've half a mind to try. There's some mystery about her I would give the world to find out. She is in with all sorts of people, even such a scamp as this, and yet she has the manners of a duchess and the bearing of a queen. Perhaps if I knew her real history I could master her. I never was beat by a woman yet. Shall I start for Boars-haven this evening, ferret it all out, and have one more try? I believe it's the dullest place in England, with the dirtiest hotel. Let me see, though: I am engaged to dinner to-day and to-morrow. Then there's Mrs. Stripwell, I promised to take her to the Alexandra Park: to be sure I could throw *her* over. Next week I might manage it; but it's a long journey, and suppose she should be gone when I get there! Besides, one *is* a gentleman, and it does seem bad form to hunt a woman down. It's unfair—hang it! unmanly! I've heard of some eastern fellow—

the Lord Mayor, Prester John, somebody—who
had a remembrancer, a wise man, to go out walking with him, and remind him of everything he
ought not to have forgotten. I've a great mind
to set up something of the kind, a fellow who
would tell me what to do when I can't settle for
myself. Now, this is a case in point,—I want to
go, and I *don't* want to go. I'd give a hundred
to see her again, and a thousand never to have
seen her at all. She has upset all my arrangements, demolished all my schemes, and, in a
roundabout way, impaired even my health. She
has vexed, baffled, and defeated me at every turn,
and yet I am hankering after her like a schoolboy. Is it because she puzzles me, or why?
I never was sure of her; never could quite make
out whether she liked me or not. No; I won't
go near her. I'll leave off being a fool. I'll give
it all up; have a final row with Mrs. Stripwell,
and retire from the business. After all, I believe
women are a mistake! I see fellows get on very

well without them. Look at Beauregard, the
handsomest man in London now, and has been
for the last twenty years; I don't believe he ever
looks at a woman, except his hideous old wife,
and he don't trouble her more than he can help.
How happy he always seems! how contented!
Dine with you, drive with you, shoot with you,
go anywhere, do anything. Now, whenever I
run off one engagement, I am obliged to pay
forfeit on another. Somebody has to be thrown
over, and then there's a blow-up. Words always; tears sometimes. Hang it—I'm sick of
the whole thing!"

Wise resolutions enough, but for such a
temperament, and after such a life, exceedingly
difficult to carry out. Habit is second nature;
and his Lordship could no more forego the excitement of flirtation than a Highlander his dram
or a Dutchman his pipe. Some men are fools
about women in early manhood, others in advanced age; but Lord St. Moritz had been

alternately their slave and tyrant his whole life
through, and perhaps in the immunity that comes
with constant danger, had taken less harm than
might have been expected, till he met Beltenebrosa.

That he regarded her with feelings more like
real attachment than those he entertained for
any of his other loves, may be inferred from the
indecision he now felt as to his movements, and
his dread of her scorn when he should appear in
his true colours. For a moment he almost made
up his mind to ask her to marry him point-blank;
but he knew himself well enough to be sure that
her very consent would make him cease to desire
it; whereas a refusal—and he had every reason
to expect one—could only render him more
devotedly and uncomfortably attached to her
than before.

There are deep meanings in the old myths
of Greece, invented by sages who sifted human
nature to the husks. No glances are so eager as

those cast on fruit hanging one hand's-breadth
out of reach; no thirst is so burning as that
which waters lips, but never slakes. Tantalus,
close under the heavy-laden boughs, up to his
neck in a running stream, must have been an
object of pity to gods and men!

Lord St. Moritz, alas! was never satisfied to
drink from his own cistern, and inherited so much
of his character from our common mother, that
having access to all the trees in the garden, he
was sure to long, like Eve, for that which bore
the forbidden fruit!

All the way home, through the rattle of a
Hansom cab, his good and evil angels argued
the point. It was hard to give her up; it was
cruel to hunt her down. No gentleman should
persist in his advances to a woman when he sees
they are unwelcome; but again, she admires
perseverance, as she appreciates fidelity, and a
breach incessantly battered must become practi-
cable at last. Scores of proverbs, contradicting

each other, were summoned to strengthen opposite sides of the argument. " If she will, she
will, you may depend on't ; and if she won't,
she *won't*, and there's an end on't ! " seemed a
doggerel replete with wisdom, till he reflected
that " constant dropping wears away a stone,"
and that the Scotch, a wise and cautious nation,
protest " nineteen nay-says make half a grant."

He was in a state of extreme vaccillation and
uncertainty about an expedition to Boarshaven ;
but perhaps, altogether, only wanted an excuse
to go.

When he reached his own house, he found it
on the hall table, in the shape of a letter from a
great lady, who has not appeared personally in
these pages, but of whom I have taken the
liberty to make mention, under her title of
Marchioness. From his Lordship's valet, who
did not fail to peruse this communication when
he took his master's coat down to brush, I gather
its contents were as follows :

"DEAR LORD ST. MORITZ,—I know how wedded you are to London, and that you find great difficulty in tearing yourself away from its *many* attractions; but I venture to hope we can persuade you to pay us a little visit next week, the 20th or 21st, just as it suits, and we trust you will stay as long as you feel the country air does you good. There is nothing else to offer. Shooting is over; the hunting, I fancy, *atrocious;* and, thank Heaven! we have no neighbours. There will be a Function at Boarshaven, a place you never heard of, but our nearest town, where we are very great people indeed: a sort of tea for the school-children, romps, and prizes, and a parson to do the polite. You know the kind of thing, and need not go if it bores you. *We* must, as it is rather a stronghold of Ned's voters, and one has to keep up the family interest. I was in hopes the ballot would have spared one all these worries, but nothing seems to make any difference. An election costs as much money, and everybody drinks as much beer, as in the good old times. I haven't heard a word of scandal for six weeks, and positively *thirst* for news, so mind you bring down a fresh budget.

"If you come, as I *hope* you will, Stoke-Erith is our station ; it is close to the North Lodge, and we will send for you, of course. If anybody asks after me, say I'm not dead yet, only *buried*, and believe me, dear Lord St. Moritz,

"Yours very sincerely,

"Rose Erith.

"P.S.—Tilbury bids me tell you he has some *dry* champagne he wants you to taste. I think it *very* nasty ! "

The valet wondered why she should still call her old Marquis by his second title, more particularly as her own marriage took place nearly twenty years after his father's death. Lord St. Moritz, who was accustomed to such confusion of nomenclature, sat promply down to write a joyful acceptance, specifying his day and the train that would bring him, promising, more over, all the stray morsels of scandal he could glean, while regretting the crop of evil was unusually scanty. So unnatural a state of things could not last, he thought. Nothing really shocking had taken place for two months. An explosion must surely be due, and no doubt it would come off before he left town next week.

CHAPTER LIV.

HUNTED.

THE bloodhounds were on her track, and though Beltenebrosa was no timid hind, to give up all hope of resistance when she ceased to find safety in flight, she had yet lost much of the self-confidence that used to support her in earlier years; she was beginning to desire security and repose,—something to trust, something to lean on, something to love. The bare idea that Jericho was following her up seemed so distasteful, she almost resolved to leave England for the Continent, and, taking with her the recommendations to which she felt justly entitled, enter on a fresh career of usefulness and good works, under another name, in a foreign country, where she might hope to remain unmolested and unknown.

That Lord St. Moritz should have joined in the chase was a turn of worse luck than she could have anticipated. It needed a painful effort of self-command to retain her calm bearing and characteristic dignity when she came face to face with him, of all places on earth, in Boarshaven infant-school, cleared out and arranged for a tea party of little people, with ruddy cheeks and wistful eyes, to be made happy in a surfeit of cake, toffee, and buns.

It was the merest chance that she found herself there at all, having by no means intended to assist at any festive gathering in her deep mourning and confirmed despondency; but the schoolmistress had been taken ill at the last moment; the Matron, who had promised to assume a divided command, was sadly at a loss for a colleague, and, knowing they could both be spared from the hospital, now nearly empty, entreated Mrs. Paravant to come forward and stand in the gap.

"It would be very hard lines for Mr. Strange," she argued, "if all his arrangements should fall through at the last moment; he set such store by these little folks, and loved to see them enjoy themselves. She had heard him say many a time that it was his one chance of holiday-making in the whole year."

This seemed a good reason, no doubt, but I am not satisfied it would have ensured compliance, had Beltenebrosa known she was to meet the Marchioness and some fine friends, amongst them Lord St. Moritz, at so homely a treat. She naturally concluded the party would consist of a hundred small tea-drinkers, the Matron of the hospital herself, and Mervyn Strange. She saw him so seldom now, it would be a joy to hear him speak, to breathe the same air, in the same room, and attend to the same duties. He would

surely not refuse to exchange a few words on
their mutual occupations, and she might even
take that opportunity of asking him in what way
she had given him offence, so low had her pride
fallen! What did it matter now? What did
anything matter? She must make up her mind
to go away, and never see him again. So she
sleeked her black locks even more carefully than
usual, put on a clean collar and cuffs, looked at
her own beautiful face in the glass, with a satisfaction of which sorrow itself could not deprive
her, and took up a position behind an enormous
tea-urn at the end of a table twenty feet long,
prepared for any eventuality, except, perhaps,
that which actually arrived.

The examination was over. It had, indeed,
to be ignominiously curtailed, wanting its usual
leader. These students of tender years could
not be expected to answer questions put in a
stranger's voice; and the curate, who was fond
of his little charges, soon saw the necessity of

letting them down easy in the matter of simple
arithmetic, short spelling, with history, natural,
sacred, and profane. So the little people clapped
their hands to a certain chorus repeated at in-
tervals to keep them awake during school-hours,
and sang a hymn, approved, doubtless, by the
angels in heaven, but quite unintelligible to
mortals on earth.

The spectators, delighted to get off with so
short a programme, voted the whole institution
" charming," reflecting the highest credit on the
management, the clergyman, and above all the
Patroness, Lady Erith, who never came near it
but on such occasions, once a year!

She entered the tea-room with her party,
at the head of a column nearly one hundred
strong, and literally gasped in astonishment to
see Mrs. Paravant superintending an array of
metal teapots, and stacks of bread and butter
two feet high.

" Good gracious, my dear!" exclaimed her

Ladyship, when she recovered breath, "I say again, emphatically, *good gracious!* What is this? What does it mean? Are you doing it for a bet?"

The other, taking Lady Erith's proffered hand, dropped a mocking little curtsey.

"You cannot be more surprised than I am," said she; "I never expected we should meet here. But your Ladyship is on duty, I conclude, and I am *not.*"

"Duty?" repeated the other. "Wait till I collect my scattered intellects. Duty? Yes, I suppose I am. It has been anything but pleasure, my dear, till I saw *you.* Now let us attend to business. Where are you staying? and when are you coming to *us?*"

The procession had been brought to a deadlock in the sudden stoppage of its leader: the children gazed at this tall handsome lady, who seemed so intimate with that absolute divinity, the Marchioness, with open-mouthed admiration.

The bystanders looked on, wondering, awestruck, and certain of the townspeople, who knew Mrs. Paravant as the mysterious sick-nurse, began to think they had "entertained an angel unawares."

Only Mervyn Strange cast restless glances at those two striking figures in juxtaposition over the tea-table, and marvelled why he had not yet reconciled himself to the conviction that Beltenebrosa and he moved in spheres wide as the poles apart. It might have been for his especial behoof she avowed her intentions to Lady Erith so decidedly and in so audible a voice.

"I have been here some weeks," said she; "but of course," glancing at her black sleeve, "I could go nowhere. Now I am packing up to start again. It is a great piece of good luck to have caught this glimpse of you at the last moment."

"You can't possibly go without paying us a visit at Stoke-Erith," insisted her Ladyship.

"Tilbury would tear his grey hair. He raves about you still. My dear, you shall be as quiet as you like. We have nobody with us—at least, nobody that *counts*—except Lord St. Moritz, and you know *him* so well. Here he is!"

She moved aside to make way for his Lordship, who advanced with extended hand, but an undecided expression of face.

"You haven't forgotten me, I hope, Mrs. Paravant," said he. "It is not so very long since we met."

"I have *not* forgotten Lord St. Moritz," she answered, in tones of icy displeasure, utterly ignoring his attempt at a cordial greeting, "nor do I wish to be reminded of him." And she turned to her teacups with an air of superiority and dignified displeasure that crushed him to the earth.

"He looked like a fool," said Lady Erith subsequently, relating this passage of arms to her kind old husband. "It was as good as a

play. You never saw anything so well done.
Our friend, as we all know, is not easily set
down, but she fairly walked over him, and I
don't think he has recovered it yet."

To tell the truth, Lord St. Moritz for once
in his life lost his head, and accepted the false
position in which he had placed himself with as
little tact as a schoolboy. In private combat
there are many ways of conducting a hand-to-
hand engagement with a lady. Some men affect
a cool superiority they by no means feel; some
rave and storm more furiously than the enemy,
silencing her, as it were, by a better sustained
fire than her own ; some again, and these, I have
been told, are more successful than might be
supposed, burst into tears, with unusual demon-
strations of emotion, and by a timely appeal to
her clemency, conquer even in the moment of
submission : but when she declares war in public
a man should lay down his arms on the spot.
He is fighting with his hands tied; the sym-

pathics of the crowd are against him; he has
not a chance, and the sooner he gets off the field
the better—pell-mell, right-about-face, and run
for your lives! All this nobody knew better
than Lord St. Moritz, yet was he so ill advised
in his vexation as to hover round Beltenebrosa,
among her cups and saucers, persistently endeavouring to attract her attention and engage
her in conversation, however commonplace, on
the homely duties of her task. Here, however,
he met with his match. Nothing he could do or
say had the slightest effect in breaking through
her haughty reserve, and if compelled to accept
his assistance, in such matters as the removal of
trays or replenishment of milk-cans, she took no
more notice of her coadjutor than of the domestic
articles he held in his hands.

"She treats me like a footman," thought his
Lordship, "and I believe I like her none the
worse! It won't last, of course. She couldn't
be so savage if she didn't care for me a little.

To-morrow there will be a reaction, and I shall sail in triumphantly on the turn of the tide!"

But here, trusting, perhaps, over-confidently to a practical knowledge of the sex, his Lordship was grossly in error. There is no such fallacy as to determine the conduct of any one woman in a particular case by some general law considered applicable to the whole sex.

What says the Preacher, the wisest of men, and unusually experienced—if we are to believe history—in such matters? "One man among a thousand have I found, but a woman among those have I not found!" meaning, I take it, that in the former sex only could some clue be afforded, by study of the many, to the character of one. To judge by his writings, women must have puzzled the royal sage exceedingly. The more he knew of them, the lower they seem to have fallen in his opinion; but perhaps, in an extensive polygamy, he may have undervalued all because he never became thoroughly acquainted

p 2

with a single individual, and fell into the vulgar error of trying to account, on known principles, for anything they professed to do, or did, or did *not!*

Lord St. Moritz, who resembled Solomon in this one respect alone, bore his disgrace as best he might—very badly indeed; made himself troublesome, made himself obnoxious, nay, made himself ridiculous—worst and most fatal mistake of all!

Few of us can have failed to remark an in-stinct of the female sex, like that of small birds in presence of a hawk, which impels them to make common cause, on certain established occasions, against the common foe. Dislikes, rivalries, even jealousies, are forgotten. They stand by their colours with an *esprit de corps* and a loyalty that defy attack. When thus massed, as it were, to "resist cavalry," in which manœuvre they are not always singly so success-ful, the enemy hovers round these fair Amazons to no purpose, retiring at last, in disorder and disgust, from the unequal fight.

Lady Erith, with feminine acuteness, detected her friend's intention of pouring discomfiture on the offending head of Lord St. Moritz, and helped her to the utmost. Even when the feast was over and the cake eaten, when rosy little mouths had been wiped, chubby little hands joined in such simple thanksgiving as flies up through the air like a rocket, and the room cleared for a distribution of prizes, to be succeeded by romps and sugar-plums, she placed Mrs. Paravant next herself, in a corner by the wall, and so hemmed her in that common good breeding forbade the most persistent of tormentors to exchange a word with her, good or bad.

"I must make the most of you while I've got you," whispered her Ladyship. "But do tell me, dear, in confidence, of course, what on earth is the meaning of it all?"

In a few hurried sentences Beltenebrosa gave

the most plausible account of herself she could evolve at such short notice. She had lost her husband, as Lady Erith knew, under very painful circumstances. Her whole life had been altered, and, indeed, darkened by this bereavement. She had been staying in London, but London was the loneliest place in the world for a "*femme seule,*" and—yes, she was sure she had been less unhappy even here at Boarshaven. Lady Erith couldn't understand that. It was not to be expected. But happiness had very little to do with *places.* For *her* part, she had given up trying for it. If she could do a little good in the world, that was all she asked. It did not much matter *where.* She had made up her mind to go abroad, because—because—she liked the hours, the climate agreed with her, and England reminded her too much of the past.

"Nonsense, my dear!" said the Marchioness; "you are hipped, bored out of health; you want tonics, gaiety, cheering up. I wish you would see *my* doctor; such a quiz, but so clever! Depend upon it, my dear, you are ill."

"Not ill," answered the other, sadly, "only unhappy."

The tears rose to her fine eyes, but Lady Erith could think of no better medicine for the mind diseased than her own panacea.

"We would soon put you to rights at Stoke-Erith," said she, rising to break up the ceremony. "Change of air, change of people, change of scene: come to-morrow," with a glance at Lord St. Moritz; "he's not going till the day after."

But his unexpected presence at this festival, combined with the dreaded arrival of Jericho Lee, had decided the intentions of Mrs. Paravant. Lady Erith knew by the pressure of her friend's hand when they parted that she meant a long farewell, and attributing this contrariety in some measure to his Lordship, was less cordial with him than usual during the whole journey home.

CHAPTER LV.

MISJUDGED.

A WOUNDED spirit seems endowed with some *clairvoyance* of its own. It sees through the eyes of the heart, at any distance and in any light, much that does exist, and also much that does *not*.

A good-natured clergyman, fond of children, superintending the wants of an infant-school at high festival of tea and cake, might be supposed to have his hands so full that he could spare little observation for matters, however engrossing, unconnected with the filling of urns, emptying of plates, and ministering to the appetites of the happy, hungry little people over whose meal he

presides. Yet did Mervyn Strange, attending
to all these details with his usual energy, detect
—through his skull, no doubt, and the back
buttons of his coat—certain grave offences in
the woman he loved, that had no existence but
in his own imagination.

It mattered little to him, he told himself,
except, of course, as challenging reproof from
one of his sacred calling, but it was evident that
this former lover had followed her here, expressly
to renew the attachment that existed, to their
shame, during her husband's life. Had not
Mrs. Tregarthen told him all about it in this
very town? and Mrs. Tregarthen, with many
faults and much love of tittle-tattle, was a shrewd,
observant, far-seeing woman of the world. He
was not inclined to believe a word at first, so
prejudiced had he been—and no wonder—in
favour of an offender whose beauty precluded
his impartial verdict, but he *must* believe his own
eyes—or rather the eyes in his waist-buttons—

now! They were flirting! Yes, that was the word used by designing men and unprincipled women to express the insidious advances of temptation—flirting egregiously, even here, in the presence of these children, whose innocent little faces should have shamed them into the pretence if not the practice of decency and virtue.

And what was he, this man?—this Lord St. Moritz, on whom the policy of our British Constitution conferred hereditary distinction as a legislator of his country? Had he any earthly merit or good quality whatever, save a reputation for that spurious wit which is more properly called insolence, and those trivial accomplishments that, as they seldom accomplish sterling worth, are rather to be deplored than envied or admired? God forbid he should judge harshly! but charity herself must not ignore truth; and that is wilful blindness, amounting to complicity, which ignores the wolf when he wears his sheep's clothing avowedly in jest.

It was no affair of his, he could not repeat too often ; but he had made inquiries concerning this nobleman, and had received much the same answer from all. His character seemed well known to be utterly devoid of principle where women were concerned. Society held up its hands in comic deprecation, and declared, upon its word, he was too bad ! His conversation was agreeable enough — " *Voyez-vous ? C'était son métier* "—but his morals were really beyond toleration, and his attentions to any lady, married or single, simply meant destruction to her fair fame.

This was the profligate whom Beltenebrosa had selected, doubtless from amongst many others, for an intimate friend—nay, a favoured admirer—before her husband's death ; and now, when the poor fellow was scarcely cold in his grave, here he stood in compromising attendance on the widow, with his silver tongue, his silken manners, and his front of brass. It was shameful, sinful, outrageous—and he blamed *her* even more than her lover. How should a woman be so lost to all sense of decency and self-respect? As a member of a Christian community, he could not sufficiently condemn her conduct. As a minister of a Christian church, he doubted but that it was his duty to protest against it aloud.

What a position would have been his own at this moment, had he not resolved long ago to tear out of his heart this folly that had so nearly conquered him! It seemed providential that he should have so schooled and prepared himself for his present trial. If happiness were gone for ever, at least duty and honour remained. Why, oh, why were these so inadequate to fill the void in his aching breast?

He knew, but would not admit, that never in his life, had he felt so miserable as when he returned to his lonely lodging from the infant-school; but a manly nature only hardens under affliction, and the more he suffered, the firmer grew his determination, neither to bend, nor quail, nor cry out, nor yield an inch!

Lady Erith too was much exercised in mind concerning her handsome friend. Considering how little they had seen of each other—perhaps for that very reason—the Marchioness had contracted a marvellous affection for this mysterious woman with the dark eyes and the foreign name. She was really pleased to meet her again, concerned to observe that she seemed unhappy, and much vexed that she failed to secure her company for a friendly visit at so dull a season of the year.

Lady Erith, quoting one of the most popular wits of the day, was wont to observe, with a comical mockery of his impressive articulation, that she could " Resist anything except temptation, and bear everything except disappointment." To the last-named trial her Ladyship was exceedingly sensitive; and connecting, as I have already observed, her failure in securing the company of Beltenebrosa with the proceedings of

Lord St. Moritz, was barely civil to that nobleman the whole way home.

Her depression lasted all through dinner. "Tilbury," as she called the Marquis, doing the affable for two stupendous dowagers, on either hand, bobbed his venerable head to shoot anxious glances at his young wife, along a table laid for eighteen, studded with hothouse plants, cups, vases, and gold plate. The old butler, who had taken her into special favour from the day she entered her new home a blooming bride, came round with his "Champagne, my Lady?" (out of her turn) in vain. Not till she had swallowed a cup of strong tea in the drawing-room was her equanimity restored, and with it arrived a rush of curiosity that she resolved, at any sacrifice, to indulge.

When the gentlemen came in, she had so arranged her party that the billiard-room was empty. As Lord St. Moritz put down his coffee-cup she challenged him to a game, and walked him off for an uninterrupted interview, during which, to use her Ladyship's own expression, she meant "to turn him inside-out like a glove."

"I'll take spot," said she, "and you shall give me ten. We'll string to begin."

Then she chalked her cue, and made an egregious miss.

"I thought our little love-feast went off very well to-day," observed this diplomatist. "I was immensely astonished to see Mrs. Paravant there, weren't you?"

Looking him through and through with her keen bright eyes, she detected something of insincerity and confusion in his own.

"I'm too old for the sensation," answered his Lordship, sprawling across the table to make a cannon. "At my time of life, I may be disgusted, but I can't be surprised."

"Disgusted! What a word! If you ask me, I thought *she* looked disgusted, not *you*."

"How did *I* look?"

"Defeated, baffled, put to shame, all over the place. Confess, now, Lord St. Moritz, you came down here on purpose to meet her, and it's no use."

"How can I confess anything so rude? I came here because you asked me, because it's the pleasantest country house in England, because your infant-school is a hundred strong. I'm *so* fond of babies!"

"Nonsense, Lord St. Moritz! she's a friend of mine, and I think you're using her ill."

"How, Lady Erith?"

"You know better than I can tell you. Have you not flirted with her ever since she appeared in society? have you not got her talked about, and to a certain extent compromised by your attentions? and now that her husband is dead and both are free, you have no right to turn round and leave her out in the cold."

"The other way up, if you please, Lady Erith. Short of boxing one's ears, she could not have snubbed me more heartily than she did to-day."

Lady Erith burst out laughing. "I admit the snub," said she, pocketing the red, which left her nothing to play for: "I never saw a more complete set-down; but it's your own fault, and it serves you right! Now listen, Lord St. Moritz. I asked her to come here before you went away, and she refused. That's nothing. I shouldn't mind going for her myself to-morrow, and carrying her off by main force, only, *mind*, if you don't mean fairly by her, and settle it all before you leave this house, I'll never speak to you again, there! It's your turn to play."

Placing the red ball on the spot, he had time to consider the situation. His Lordship did not at all fancy being taken possession of in so high-handed a fashion, and this eagerness on the part of his hostess to see him married was exceedingly unflattering, as arguing not on her own account the slightest partiality for him.

"I am obliged to go away to-morrow, my dear Lady Erith," said he. "It is most unfortunate, but I had a telegram this afternoon, requiring me back in town. I have had such a pleasant visit, and only regret it could not be longer. But you'll ask me again, won't you?"

"That depends. I daresay Tilbury will. Do you mean to marry my black friend, and become a respectable man?"

"Don't you think I'm nicer as I am?"

There was something so absurdly cool and imperturbable in the rejoinder, that she could not help laughing, though intensely provoked, and his Lordship played the game out, feeling that once more the collar had been nearly slipped over his head, but he had escaped.

"Depend upon it, Rosie," said the Marquis, when in the sanctity of her dressing-room she related this encounter to the kind old husband, whose experience of the world and its ways had sharpened his faculties, but by no means hardened his heart, "you had better have let it alone. St. Moritz knows what he is about, and it's possible he may not consider your handsome favourite, whom I think charming myself, so fit to be a wife as you do. He has had great opportunities of judging, you must remember."

"That's exactly what I say. It's the very reason I want him to do her justice."

"No doubt, my dear," was the placid reply; "but you cannot expect *him* to see it quite from the same point of view."

So Beltenebros not only fell in the good opinion of the man she loved, but also lost her friends' support, through the events of the day; and yet how could she have conducted herself with more womanly reserve, more propriety of conduct, from first to last?

As no man's character, however unblemished, is high enough to escape calumny, so no woman can hope to go through the world uninjured by the malice of her enemies, but more especially uncondemned by the verdict of her friends.

It is so easy to blame; so easy and so pleasant withal, inferring a nice discrimination, an exalted standard, and a conscious moral superiority. People who have never handled a brush, steered a ship, or set a squadron in the field, have no hesitation in laying down the law on the defects of a portrait and the incompetency of a hero by land or sea. Those whose hearts are mere organs of animal economy, that have never ached with sorrow nor swelled with sentiment, sit in judgment, usually damnatory, on the poor sufferer, whose tortures have proved unbearable only because of the sensitive generous disposition they wrong so cruelly. Everybody sees the beam in his neighbour's eye, nobody puts himself in his neighbour's place.

" She loves him with a criminal attachment," argued Mervyn Strange. " They understand

each other, and that affected coolness in public
is to deceive the world."

"I suppose I ought to drop her," pondered
Lady Erith. "I'm not censorious, and she's *a
dear;* but one *must* draw the line somewhere,
and from Lord St. Moritz's manner, I am half
afraid there is something wrong."

CHAPTER LVI.

STRANGERS YET.

I DO not conceive that in those mental sufferings, which seem the very conditions, more or less severe, of a soul's training for immortality, any torture can be greater than that which racks two loving hearts, yearning to come together, but separated by a gulf known only to themselves, purely imaginary, yet none the less impassable and profound. The chains that bind them are invisible and impalpable as those of the nightmare, when she ties us hand and foot, paralysing every sensation but that of fear. The moment of waking no doubt sweeps them away, as a morning breeze sweeps its film from the

meadow ; but no dreamer can rouse *himself*, and
it needs a friendly hand, often rudely applied, to
bring him back to the regions of reality and
common sense.

There was no kindly go-between to reconcile
Beltenebrosa and Mervyn Strange. No impartial
counsellor to tell them what fools they were, and
how, from a sense of false pride and fancied in-
jury, they threw to the winds that chance of
happiness which is said to come for each of us
once in a lifetime, and no more.

They dwelt in adjoining streets, less than a
hundred yards apart. They met ten times a
day. On occasion they could not avoid ex-
changing ceremonious greetings, even a few
commonplace words. Great heavens ! It is
enough to drive a man mad, that he must pro-
pound platitudes about the weather, telling the
woman he loves " it is a fine day," when he
longs to fall at her feet and never get up again
till she takes him to her breast ! And for *her :*

do you suppose she does not suffer too? though
with more outward calmness and a better grace,
as looking forward presently in her own chamber
to the relief of tears—a solace denied to the
stronger sex.

Beltenebrosa, perhaps from her wilder nature,
seemed more impatient of sorrow than the curate,
and decided, with characteristic impetuosity, that
she would bear it no longer.   There were other
places in the world besides Boarshaven, which
was, moreover, no secure refuge now.   She must
leave it without delay, and so, at a bold stroke,
put an end to this suspense and misery, once for
all.

She would have gone without wishing
Strange good bye—so she told herself—had it
not been that a recommendation in his own
hand, testifying to her efficiency as a nurse,
might be advantageous to her future career.
After all, she argued, she had done nothing to
be ashamed of.   Though he chose to avoid her

so cruelly, there was no earthly reason why they ought not to meet. And it would be something to take with her into banishment : the last word, the last look of the man she loved so dearly.

Yes, she did not try to conceal it from herself. The impression made by Mervyn Strange on her girlhood, at first so slight that she sacrificed him without a scruple, had deepened, day by day and week by week, as she advanced to maturity, till at last in the prime of her womanhood—none the less because it seemed he could never be her own—she had established him as the ideal of her intellect, the chosen of her heart.

Only a woman can understand how she must have loved him, to hoard away the amount of her debt, and keep it in reserve, that she might pay him at any moment, hesitating to do so only because it seemed to constitute a community of interest, and she could not bear to sever this the last link between them with her own hand. So

the day after the school-feast, Beltenebrosa prepared herself by a careful toilet for the final
interview she was resolved to extort. All her
appliances of dress and decoration were well
chosen, we may be sure; and though mourning
affords no great scope for indulgence of the
fancy, there are many little coquetries of costume
exceedingly fascinating in black. If we may be
pardoned a bad pun, weeds will sometimes do
your business quite as effectually as flowers.

I am firmly persuaded that no true woman
would neglect to set her bonnet straight if her
head were going to be cut off the next minute.
And this regard to externals is, in my opinion,
one of the most valuable qualities of the sex.
What would they be without vanity? What *are*
they in the privacy of domestic life, when familiarity has bred conjugal contempt, and the wife,
careless of her husband's admiration, sinks into
a slattern, while she sours to a shrew? No!
Vanity, in a good-looking woman, is one of her

greatest charms, and in an ugly one, if such exist, what is it but a healthy corrective and reminder—the leaven that leavens the whole lump?

Exceedingly brave at a distance, and confident in her armour of proof, Beltenebrosa felt her heart sink wofully while she approached the curate's home. It spared her some embarrassment, and perhaps a sharp conflict with her own self-respect, to meet him in the street, walking sadly along, and scanning the pavement with an air of unusual dejection. A moment's consideration, she felt, would put her to flight in disorder; so, dashing forward with the courage of despair, she got into line, as it were, and charged forthwith.

"Good bye, Mr. Strange," said she, advancing on him with a slender black-gloved hand held out. "I was coming to say it in your own house, but it will do as well here. I'm going away on Monday morning early. Good bye!"

Why should he care?　Why should the simple conventional farewell sound in his ear like a knell for the dead?　Going away!　Of course she was.　To Stoke-Erith; to the Marchioness and her fashionable friends; to Lord St. Moritz and his detestable attentions.　He expected as much, just as he might have expected the shock of a shower-bath when he pulled the string; but it took his breath away all the same!

"Good bye, Mrs. Paravant," he rejoined, stiffly enough, accepting, rather than taking, the offered hand.　"Make my compliments, if you please, to the Marchioness.　I have written to thank her for kindly attending yesterday; but perhaps you will say I shall take an early opportunity of paying my respects at Stoke-Erith?"

His heart was going like a sledge-hammer, but his accents were measured, even precise.　A woman, not in love with him, would have said, "This man is pompous, and a prig!"

"Stoke-Erith!" she repeated. "I am not going near Stoke-Erith. Do you think I should trouble you to say good bye for a mere drive like that? No, Mr. Strange. I mean to cross the Channel on Monday night, and—and I hope it won't be very rough."

There was something pitiful though ludicrous in the last sentence that roused his tenderest sympathies, but, with a moment's reflection, the sterner nature re-asserted itself. She was going, of course, to meet Lord St. Moritz at Paris, that easy capital where it is supposed people "can do as they like," though I believe there is no greater social fallacy than this persuasion, even if they could make up their minds what they *did* like.

"I have forgotten most of my French," said he, indifferently; "but I remember enough to say *bon voyage!*"

The wounded spirit would have cried aloud, but for the bitter indignation that "when we are wroth with those we love" acts like a styptic on a wound, and though it forces tears out of the heart, keeps them back from the eyes. She only answered in a low, mournful voice,

"You can do something for me before I go."

Why could he not tell her the truth, and state honestly that if she had asked him to cut his throat, then and there, for her amusement, he would only have been too delighted to oblige? Why cannot people say what they think, and be no less outspoken in their love than their hate? Perhaps, in destroying much uncertainty, such candour would ruin the romance of the whole thing. We should have no sighs to record, no dreams, no drawbacks, no disappointments; and to write a three-volume novel would be simply impossible.

The curate bowed austerely enough, and waited for information.

"I require a written recommendation from *you*, Mr. Strange," continued Beltenebrosa, in rather haughty accents, and with her head up, " countersigned, if you please, by the Matron of your hospital, setting forth my capabilities as a nurse. You cannot refuse to do me this justice, nor, I hope, would you wish to hinder me on the path I have chosen for myself."

While he pictured her in a foreign country, friendless, alone, ministering in fever wards or pestilent *faubourgs*, he had much ado to refrain from a scene in the public streets; but the hated image of Lord St. Moritz came to his assistance, and arguing that these weaker sentiments were part of the temptation he was bound to resist, he gained the mastery with a strong effort, but determined to prolong the contest no further. Lifting his hat with scrupulous courtesy, he observed, "I will send it round to you this evening," walked gravely into the house, and shut the door.

He never invited her to enter. He had not so much as asked her to sit down, thought Beltenebrosa, and it was obviously his intention to avoid her even now, on this the last occasion they would be together on earth. Perhaps it was better so, she said to herself with somewhat bitter resignation. It made her task lighter, her duty less irksome. In proof how much easier it seemed to leave him, she buried her face in her handkerchief the instant she was round the corner, and sobbed as if her heart would break. The tears would only have flowed more freely, perhaps, could she have seen the man she loved wrestling with his agony in the privacy of his own study, praying to be delivered from temptation on his bended knees.

CHAPTER LVII.

LATE FOR CHURCH.

THERE is no feeling of anger more self-sustaining than that which the Latin poet calls " *Spretæ injuria formæ.*" But it takes diverse shapes. It goaded Dido to self-destruction, and I fear that in these modern days it has driven many a poor girl in a ragged petticoat to jump from the parapet of Waterloo Bridge. Amongst ladies of fashion, happily, it seldom gains such mastery as to induce these desperate expedients. A beauty in good society, flouted by one lover, generally revenges herself *on* herself, in a far pleasanter manner, by taking another.

Some, indeed, do not even wait for this excuse; and we are all acquainted with charming people, friends, no doubt, of Mrs. Stripwell, who change their admirers less often, perhaps, than their dresses, but more often than their doctors; these seem to have established an excellent rule for female immunity. They never allow the man to tire first; and of such versatile mistresses, though it speaks little for his good sense, the man seldom tires at all!

Alas for Beltenebrosa! that, with those outward graces of the fashionable world she learned so readily, her force of character and keen temperament forbade her to acquire such hardness of heart as affords a woman the only real armour of proof when she goes down to battle with the world. Seeing her move through a drawing-room, with the carriage and bearing of a queen, who would have suspected the strong, unbridled feelings that tore her heart beneath that proud exterior, or detected the wild, sensitive gipsy nature under the finished manner and assumed indifference of a fine lady before the world?

It is positively awful to reflect on the contrast between people as they seem, and people as they are! There is, perhaps, no such disillusion as to meet an actress off the stage. She disappoints you—and it is saying a great deal,—even more than a theatre by daylight; but what in her is the disuse of rouge, whiting, and stage decoration, compared to the abandonment of that conventional propriety which every woman wears habitually in presence of her nearest and dearest, as of society in general; but, attacked by sorrow, sickness, or strong excitement, takes off in the privacy of her own chamber, when she puts on a dressing-gown, and lets down her back hair?

It is wonderful to reflect, literally and metaphysically, how very much the best of us are made up of clothes, after all!

"Scrape the Russian," said Napoleon, "and you come to the Tartar." Even so inside her silks and cambrics, nay, under the very coating of enamel that plates a haughty dame of modern fashion, beats a heart as fond, reckless, and unreasonable as ever impelled to crime the squaw in her wigwam, or the gipsy in her tent. She can love blindly as a savage, and, I imagine, if crossed or flouted, you need not scrape very deep to find in her also something of the Tartar.

Beltenebrosa, cast off by the man she loved, was a prey to mingled feelings of vexation, disappointment, and wounded pride. Had she not been going away she might have held her own well enough, returning scorn for scorn, and assuming an indifference no less unreal, while far better acted, than his own. But even as imaginary grievances and commonplace differences vanish in the presence of death, so she found no room in her heart for any feeling but deep sorrow and contrition in the prospect of a parting that she told herself was to wither and destroy for ever her hopes, her future, all the bloom and promise of her youth. Winter seemed to have come before she had done with spring, and night to have overtaken her in the very flush of day.

It was a miserable Sunday. Boarshaven had been too well provided with bells, from a full and complete peal at St. Bede's to a little cracked monitor that summoned half a dozen cobblers and an insane baker to hear each other discourse by turns in a meeting-house called the Ichabod. These were all set jangling at once. Beltenebrosa, packing up with a heavy heart, was fain to stop her ears that she might exclude the jarring sounds, each of which seemed to beat like a hammer on her brain. At breakfast—such a mockery of a breakfast!—an envelope arrived containing the recommendation she had asked for. No letter; not even a simple little note. She shook the cover out over and over again— only two lines at the edge: " With good wishes and prayers for your welfare.—M. S."

She never looked at the document. She

leaned her head on her hands, and knew that she suffered and tried to be strong. It would have been the longest day she ever spent, but that she grudged every passing moment as hurrying her nearer to her doom, and though each seemed to bring with it a fresh pang, yet the dusk of evening arrived all too soon.

Her resolution gave way. She would see him again—not speak to him, of course, but look in his face once more, and hear his voice. She had not been to church all day. She would go to evening service at St. Bede's, where he was to preach a charity sermon on behalf of his favourite hospital. She would sit in a dark corner, far away from the pulpit, and watch and listen, and try to think of heaven—not *him !*

It was strange how she looked forward to this inadequate consolation. What store she set by it! How it seemed to postpone her departure, and put to-morrow much farther off. So she started in good time, when it had been dark about an hour, for she meant to be early, so as not to lose one of the moments that were now so precious and slipped away so fast.

At her own door she met Nance, completely recovered in body, but obviously much distressed in mind. A policeman would have judged such strong emotion in one so shabbily dressed the result of inebriety; but Beltenebrosa knew her gipsy kinswoman better, and even in that dim lamplight could distinguish the quick restless glance of terror from the vague uncertainty of drink.

" I must speak to you, sister," whispered Nance, whose face was deadly pale, while her black hair hung down to her waist. " Not here, not here! He'll knife me, as sure as you're born! Come into the dark—up yonder, beyond the market-place! "

The woman seemed almost frightened out of her wits. Her words came thick and hoarse. She wiped her clammy forehead, and the slender dirty hand she laid on the arm of her listener shook like a leaf.

"Who will knife you?" asked Beltenebrosa, not without uncomfortable misgivings, for of all disorders, fear is the most contageous: "not Jericho? Have you seen him?"

"Speak low," muttered the other, in shaking accents. "He's one of those as can hear plain at a mile off. No, not Jericho — though *he* wouldn't think twice about it if he knowed where I was now—it's my Zachary, as swears if ever I was to split on him he'd swing for me, he would! And he'll not go back from his word. We're safe enough in this out-of-the-way corner, but we must speak low, sister, even here!"

They had entered a dark, ill-conditioned street, without a single lamp, of which a few hovels rather than houses, and the dead wall of a brewery, formed the sides. Any windows that looked on it were shuttered. Not a footfall was to be heard. They could not have been more alone on the top of a mountain.

"It's you that must do it!" whispered Nance, excitedly. "There's nobody else in the world as can. It's a rough job, but he's got to be told, sister, and by *you!*"

"He! Who?"

"Why, that there long parson—the best gentleman on God's earth, I don't care who the other is! The man as lifted me up out of this very dirt here beneath our feet, and took as much care of *me*—Gipsy Nance—as if it had been the daintiest lady in the land. Ay! and he'd come to my bed-side, whiles I was down in the fever, and speak good words, such as I didn't think it was in the tongue of a man to get out. I'm a sight more used to banning and cursing, you know, at home. What do you think, sister? He told me my life were as precious, and my soul—for he said he was sure as I'd got one— ay, precious as even the ¦Queen's on her throne, and had cost as much too, though I didn't clearly make out why. And am I to let that there angel be put upon, and ill used, robbed, and maybe murdered—yes, *murdered*, sister!— for my Zachary sticks at nothing, nor Jericho neither, once their knives are out. Not if I knows it! I wish the hair may fall from my head, and the teeth drop out of my mouth, and my hands rot off at the wrists first!"

She seemed to gather courage in talking, and Beltenebrosa, who suspected danger to her idol, felt no more fear for herself now than a lioness defending her whelps.

"Steady, Nance!" she said, in a low, firm voice, laying her hand on the other's arm. "What am I to do? Tell me all you know."

"What you've got to do is to warn of him. *Now*, sister, this very night as he goes home from church," replied Nance. "Oh! it's a good plant enough, but they little thought as I'd come in and gone upstairs, and heard every word, putting my ear against the floor. Bless ye, sister, I'm that quick of ear, I can almost hear the snow fall! I slipped out again afore my Zachary came up, and he don't guess as I'm down to him no more than the dead. Well, they laid of it out between them, and if it had been any other man alive I wouldn't have moved a finger, good or bad; for business, you know, is business, when all's said and done. What is a Gorgio, more or less, to such as you and me? But this one? No! That's why I come here, sister, as fast as my legs could carry me; 'For,' says I, 'Jane Lee can save him,' says I, 'and Jane Lee *will* save him, for poor Nance's sake.'"

"It makes little matter for whose sake," said Beltenebrosa. "Done it must be, and that without loss of time. Steady, Nance; once more, tell me, as short as you can, what you heard of their plans. Take your own time, but not more than you can help."

Then Nance entered on a confused and rambling statement, from which Beltenebrosa, whose courage and presence of mind rose to the occasion, extracted the following facts, by a judicious cross-examination, conducted with patience deserving the highest praise.

It appeared that Jericho and Zachary, who had lately arrived at Boarshaven, having spent all their substance in drink, and being now thoroughly habituated to crime, missed no opportunity of supplying themselves with the funds they required by petty lanceny, burglary, or even robbery with violence when the prospective booty was sufficiently tempting. Pending the black mail they intended to levy from their kinswoman, into whose presence Jericho, mindful of matrimonial views, did not care to enter till he could make a more splendid appearance, these worthies hit upon a plan that seemed to promise lucrative returns, at the slight risk of an encounter, two to one, with an unarmed man.

They ascertained that Mervyn Strange was to

preach on this very Sunday evening one of those
sermons of which the eloquence is to be gauged
by the collection. His oratory—"gab" they
called it—was known to be of a persuasive nature,
and the contributions of his congregation would
probably amount to several pounds. He would
carry it all with him to his lodgings, preparatory
to defraying certain expenses and paying the
balance into a county bank next day. Their
information as to these details was professionally
correct, and they had studied every inch of the
ground he would traverse between the church
door and his own home.

In a dark narrow passage called Crone's
Alley it would be easy enough to surprise and
overpower him. Strong knuckles pressed into
his neck under the ears would stifle any outcry;
and if he *did* show fight, being, though slight,
a lengthy muscular man, why, a push with the
knife made less noise and was neater practice
than all the vulgar bludgeons and thumpings in

the world. If he wore a watch, they promised each other not to take it; the money they *would* have, because gold and silver could not be traced. Nothing else; not even his sermon, Jericho protested, with grim facetiousness. They would leave him his bread-winner to get more.

"Why didn't you go to the police?" asked Beltenebrosa; for such formidable disclosures seemed more adapted to the ear of a vigilant inspector than a young woman proceeding quietly to evening church.

"Police!" repeated Nance, scornfully; "and been run in, maybe, on a charge of drunkenness, to be locked up till it was all over; and then dragged before the Beak to swear away my Zachary's life, or his liberty, at best—'cause I doesn't suppose as they'd let him count for a regular husband, not by law,—help him to the hulks, maybe, or the House of Correction; starve for want while he is in, and likely get my throat cut when he comes out! No, no, sister; I've done all I dare—told you all I know. You may take it or leave it: I won't meddle nor make with it no more!"

They separated while she spoke, hurrying off in opposite directions, and Beltenebrosa found herself in a few minutes at the door of St. Bede's, causing some little stir and observation by her late entrance. He was safe enough for the present, at any rate,—tall and stately between the lamps, in his white surplice, reading with impressive gravity the portion of Scripture appointed for the evening lesson. She heard not a syllable: she was thinking of the touching parable that describes how a certain wayfarer fell among thieves.

CHAPTER LVIII.

"MARTHA."

WAS it counted to her for sin that she could not
fix her attention on the prayers of our beautiful
Liturgy, nor draw from its soothing phrases that
consolation which it seems to afford the most
restless and preoccupied of worshippers? We
humbly hope not. If, like Martha, she seemed
so cumbered with terrestrial matters that she had
no thought to spare for heavenly things, hers at
least was an emergency that made such negli-
gence pardonable: as when a poor dumb creature falls into a pit, and man extricates it in
common humanity on the Sabbath Day.

Once, during the anthem, she felt her spirit rise for a few brief moments, on the floating notes, into those realms of eternal peace,—that promised land, longed for, now and again, by the most worldly of us, " where the wicked cease from troubling, and the weary are at rest ; " but when the peal of the organ died away, she came down to earth again, and the welfare of Christendom, the approval of angels, the kingdom of heaven itself, seemed as nothing, compared with the one life that was at stake to-night. She tried to fix her thoughts, she tried to repent of her sins, she tried hard to pray, but her mute petition, such as it was, went up in ceaseless iteration, " Save him ! save him ! If a sacrifice be required, make *me* the victim, and let him go free ! "

Like a thorough woman, she had acted on impulse rather than reflection, flying to guard her beloved with the instinct that causes a hen to ruffle round her brood. It would have been wiser, perhaps, to have gone to the police station, on the chance of obtaining aid from one of the four constables supposed to coerce into good behaviour twice as many thousand inhabitants, and eaten her heart with impatience while she waited at the locked door of an empty office; but it never occurred to her, perhaps fortunately for the object of attack, to claim protection from the civil power; and if he was threatened by personal danger, it seemed only her *right* to be at his side.

All this, notwithstanding she had yesterday bidden him an eternal farewell, and had since told herself a hundred times that every link was broken between them, and she had done with him for ever. Her plan seemed sensible enough. She would watch at the vestry door, from which he was sure to come out after taking off his canonicals, and implore him to shelter in his rector's house hard by, till those who had schemed to waylay him were tired of waiting.

At a later hour it would be easy to get a few stout amphibious parishioners to accompany him home. With such an escort woe to the marauder who should dare to lay a finger on "Payson." These mariners of Boarshaven, with many sterling qualities, were a roughish lot. The manly courage displayed by Mervyn Strange in cases of fever or contagious disease, and, on one occasion, in an awkward street row, had won their good opinion. They loved a fight at all times, and with so excellent an excuse as the curate's quarrel this favourite pastime would be carried out with unusual spirit. Yes; he was safe enough at any hour of the night with a Boarshaven bodyguard, and—delightful reflection!—he would owe his preservation to the woman he had scorned.

A general stir, the cough that bespeaks attention, a shuffling of feet and rustling of Bibles, denoted that the prayers were ended and the sermon about to begin. Waking out of her

s 2

dreams, rather ashamed that she should have allowed earthly interests so to engross her thoughts, Beltenebrosa saw Strange mount the pulpit, and wondered, with a longing heart, whether, in all that crowded congregation, he could have noticed the presence of so insignificant a unit as herself. The most pious of men are but mortal. Neither cassock nor cuirass can be made invulnerable, and there is no more immunity for the clergyman than the dragoon. Mervyn Strange knew she was in church as well as she did herself, and while her presence afforded him more happiness than he had ever hoped to experience again, he tried hard to realize the dignity of his office, the majesty of the Master before whom he stood, and to preach his best for the whole congregation, not for *her* alone.

So, while the deaf pew-opener took a pinch of snuff, and the clerk settled himself into an attitude of dignified criticism, he turned up his

lamps, hitched his gown on his shoulders, and
gave out his text.

It was short and simple enough, though it
contained, in a score of words, matter for a
thousand homilies, and directions for every be-
nevolent, happy, and useful life, suggesting only
that love for the brother who *is* seen must be
the best proof of love for the God who is *not*.

He seemed to hold none of those pessimist
views so popular with many excellent divines,
and neither told his congregation that this beautiful earth was a mass of festering corruption, in
which good, moral and material, was wholly
choked in evil, nor that the devil, whom they
defied, had the mastery, even here, over the
Lord whom they worshipped and tried to serve ;
unworthily indeed, and unsuccessfully, but with
humble hopeful hearts, honestly doing their best.
Every man, he said, had the materials for happiness at command, if he would but make judicious use of that which he found to his hand.

Were not their wives, their children, their homes, their very physical wants of eating and drinking, and the comforting smoke over the fire, matters affording, on the average, infinitely more pleasure than pain? and when the good turned to evil, was it not invariably and inexcusably their own fault? If the head of the house, however lowly, were always kind, courteous, and good-tempered, would the mother scold or the little ones brawl? the man who was content with his pint that did him good, and no more, suffered neither in health nor pocket; while even if want or sickness should overcome the honest, God-fearing labourer, friends rose for him here below on every side, and something in his breast consoled him with the reflection that he had the best Friend of all, the Friend who never forgets nor forsakes,—on high.

What was that something? They all had it; they all felt it. He would tell them. It was the voice of God; the still small voice; the voice

that comforted them when dying; the voice that
would bid them welcome home when dead.

No, their Maker did not intend they should
be miserable, here or hereafter.   Were there no
world but this—which God forbid!—compliance
with the laws He laid down for us was the only
sure rule for attaining mere material comfort
and happiness.   Even from a selfish point of
view, every man should do good to his brother.
He would put it rudely and familiarly thus :
Most of his hearers were men who earned their
bread and the few little luxuries they could
command by daily toil, always hard, sometimes
dangerous.   Was there one of them who could
deny he felt a certain sense of pleasure in sharing
his scanty morsel of food, his shallow drop of
drink, with a friend, or even his last bit of
tobacco, far down Channel there, at slack-water,
with a messmate?   And why?   What was the
meaning of this ?   It was the God-given instinct
which, when his Maker made man in His own

image, He breathed into the grosser clay, so as to refine it for ever with one drop of that pure essence which gives its beauty to earth as it constitutes the very atmosphere of heaven.

Yes, if they would prosper in their doings, let them be just with all; if they would be happy in themselves, let them be more than just, let them be generous, to their neighbours. And if they would fetch the post they steered for the whole long voyage through,—the wished-for fair haven—so beautiful, so peaceful, after baffling winds and sudden squalls and washing seas,—let them look well to their navigation, study their course, and, above all, investigate the chart furnished expressly for their information and guidance by One who would not fail to pilot them safely into harbour at last. Let them not mistake him. This world was never meant to be all calm and sunshine. Now the barque must beat against a whole gale, anon she is gliding through summer seas on an even keel; but the same wind that

baffles those "clearing out" fills joyously the
sails of the "homeward bound." The very sickness and sorrow of our brother here is turned
to a blessing rather than a curse, in the manly
kindness that relieves his wants, pours balm into
his sores, and sets him on his way again, as the
Good Samaritan set the hapless wayfarer rejoicing, indeed, yet not more heartily than his
benefactor, gladdened by the exercise of a charity
that blesses him who gives even more than him
who receives.

And so on, and so on, for less than twenty-
five minutes from end to end. Then the money-
box went round, returning many an auspicious
thump and jangle, as coppers poured in freely
from the very poorest—shillings, half-crowns,
and sovereigns from the well-to-do. Many an
honest toil-worn hand gave more than it had
intended. "Payson," you see, was so much in
earnest, and, as his parishioners used to observe,
said neither more nor less than he meant. They

knew him, too, and respected him personally. Such familiarity, when it breeds confidence rather than contempt, opens the purses of a congregation, I think, wider than the measured utterances of the Most Reverend Lord Bishop, in all the dignity of his office and his sleeves of lawn.

It is something to be assured that he who preaches does not fail to practise, and can show us the narrow way with all the more certainty that he treads its ups and downs himself.

Beltenebrosa had forgotten her purse, not purposely, I firmly believe, but in a preoccupation of mind that denoted she was thinking less of the sermon than the preacher, while she prepared for evening church. Had it not been so, she must have emptied all its store as a tribute to the eloquence which sent home to her not unprejudiced heart, and, but that she had such grave matters to ponder, would have felt cruelly humiliated in presence of the portly churchwarden, who seemed to take her impecuniosity as a personal affront.

Nevertheless, the collection was a good one, and amounted to a booty well worthy of such distinguished professors as Zachary Cooper and Jericho Lee. The thought of these two ruffians acted on Beltenebrosa like spurs in the sides of a generous horse, flurrying her actions, perhaps, more than they accelerated her movements. She was out of church long before Strange left the pulpit, and, shrinking behind a buttress to avoid observation, waited for him with a beating heart at the vestry door.

CHAPTER LIX.

FALLEN AMONG THIEVES.

WHY didn't he come? How slow the minutes passed! Each after each she saw the long-drawn files of the congregation emerge on their way home, some praising the sermon, some calculating its proceeds, some pondering in silence on the good seed lately sown, we may hope, to bear a hundredfold. There will be no differences of rank, we are taught, in heaven ; nor will it matter whether we take our last drive of all in a hearse or wheelbarrow, but we certainly *do* cling to our social distinctions as long as we can, and carry them with us even to church. There seems to be a scale of precedence both for entering and leaving the sacred edifice, regulated on a principle that the lowest should come and go first. Beltencbrosa, watching in her corner, counted out her fellow-Christians one by one : the old women who lived in the almshouses, the man with a wooden leg, the day labourers—single, then married; the amphibious mariners, in the same order; the sweep, with a clean face; the postman, the small shopkeepers, the principal butcher, who rented a grazing-farm ; the doctor, the banker, the rector leaning on his wife ; last of all, sexton and clerk. Still no Mervyn Strange.

Oh! if her heart would only keep quiet! She turned sick, and her brain began to swim ; but that fine organization was not going to fail at such a crisis, and though it cost no small effort, she retained her wits sufficiently to review the situation, and ask herself, why ?

The answer was simple enough : he had gone out at the other door. Could she have known what we know, she would have saved many precious moments, and spared herself much suffering. He noticed her come into church. Against its master's will, his rebellious eye rested on her form more than once during the service, and although we will not think so meanly of his self-command as to suppose that his thoughts wandered from his duty till its conclusion, there was ample time while disrobing in the vestry to appreciate and accept the temptation of one more brief meeting, only to take her hand, ask " How did you like my sermon?" and say good bye.

So he left his church by the door at which she came in, and where, indeed, she would naturally have gone out, scanning, as he threaded his retiring congregation, all its female figures, with an attention exceedingly foreign to the decorous habits of a clergyman, and when persisted in, by no means creditable to his reputation.

With a sinking heart he told himself he had missed her, and it served him right! what had he to do with such follies and weaknesses? A minister of the Gospel, and on a Sunday night, too! It was all for the best. Why should he wish to resume that chain of which the iron had entered his soul? The links were frayed and worthless now; let them part and be done with for good and all! Yet how beautiful she looked, in the semi-obscurity of that remote pew, her pale face showing like a pearl against the dusky background, while she turned her stately little head towards him with the earnest gesture he remembered only too well. How could so queenly a bearing wear the brand of dishonour? It seemed impossible! and yet——. He groaned in spirit, while he told himself that had he been a layman he would have taken her to him, shame and all; that now, though he might not so degrade his sacred office, he would ask no better than to purchase one last interview, second by second, at the price of so many drops of blood!

He walked fast in his agitation, and little

guessed how she was hurrying to overtake him, eager, resolved, breathless, praying only that she might be in time.

Fleet of foot as the wild deer, no sooner was she satisfied her watch had been at the wrong door than she started in pursuit at a pace that brought her in sight of the clergyman's tall form as it glided under a dim street-lamp to vanish in the black entrance of Crone's Alley. She redoubled her speed then. It seemed too late to save him; but the shudder with which she pictured to herself Jericho's knife rising overhead merged in a thrill of triumph at the consciousness that she could share his fate.

Never had those supple limbs borne her so fast; never had she so taxed the speed and endurance of her blood. Ere Strange was half-way down the narrow passage she had gained its mouth. Already she marked how a light at the far end showed and faded alternately with the undulations of his figure as he walked.

Suddenly the gleam disappeared, blotted out as it were and swallowed up in night. The next moment she heard a scuffle of feet, a hideous oath, and the beloved voice exclaiming in husky, choking accents,

"No! no! my friend; not while I can stand up and hit out!"

Her feet pattered like rain. In a dozen paces she was amongst them. Even in the gloom her eyes, sharpened by love and fear, took in each detail of the encounter. Mervyn Strange was yet on his legs; but dragging him backwards, clinging to his neck and shoulders as the hunting-leopard clings to its game, Zachary's short muscular figure was paralysing the efforts of their joint victim to defend himself from Jericho Lee in front.

Though anything but powerful-looking, the clergyman's lean frame, hardened by temperate habits and strong exercise, was unusually wiry and muscular, equal to long-sustained effort, and fortified by the *condition*—there is no other word for it — that is so telling even in the briefest encounter waged hand-to-hand.

As his new ally arrived, he managed to shake himself clear of Zachary, launching at the same time a backward kick that for a few seconds incapacitated the tinker, and made him yell with pain. Jericho now found his hands full. Losing his head, perhaps, for he heard the approaching footsteps, stimulated, moreover, to spurious courage and real ferocity by drink, he whipped his long knife from its sheath with a storm of oaths, and rushed in. His arm went up to strike; but it was seized by Beltenebrosa, who clung like a wild cat.

"Blast ye!" exclaimed the gipsy, mad with rage, as he recognized his kinswoman. "You would, would you? Take it, then. You ought to have had it months ago!" And he plunged the weapon once, twice, furiously in her side.

The clergyman's hand was on the villain's

throat, but his grasp relaxed as a dusky wisp of garments subsided at his feet. Zachary, who had recovered his senses, counselled instant flight.

"Morrice, Jerry!" growled the tinker, in terse, suggestive phrase. "The rest's a-comin'! And —— it! we ain't got the swag arter all!"

The curate never heard their hurrying feet, nor thought of his own narrow escape, nor remembered he had saved his treasure for the sick. He only knew that there she lay, his Beltenebrosa—yes, his very own now—bleeding her life out on the cold, wet stones in the dark.

But if the evil men do brings its own punishment, surely the good is returned to them a hundredfold. The hospital he had established at the cost of many an anxious thought, many an effort of self-abasement and self-sacrifice, did him worthy service now. In less than five minutes the motionless form of his preserver, carried thither in his own strong, loving arms, was laid in a comfortable bed expressly adapted for such emergencies, and its wounds, of which one was deep and dangerous, were being stanched by that experienced Matron who for nerve and skill seemed no whit inferior to the surgeon, sent for on the instant, to arrive in less than a quarter of an hour.

Those only can imagine how the two watchers hung upon every breath of the sufferer who have seen the life of one human being, and the hopes of another, moored by a single thread, that may part at any moment, to let the soul drift out for ever on the dark waters of the unknown. Mervyn Strange could appreciate, none better, the reality of that future to which he looked forward himself, while he taught others to believe with him, as the solace for all human sorrow, the climax of all imaginable joy. Yet none the less did the suspense of those racking minutes, while he feared that the woman he loved might get to the Happy Land before him, plough furrows in his cheek, and sprinkle his hair with snow. In years to come, when laughing children shall twine their fingers in papa's grizzled locks, the proud and happy wife who bore them will scarce keep back her tears !

Yes; there is a time for reward as there is a time for trial. Infinite Wisdom allots each in such proportion as shall bring to perfection that noblest of all creations—the human soul. Mervyn Strange had been taught, through much tribulation, that man's love for woman, refined and spiritualized by a self-sacrifice which holds it second to duty, is a divine ordinance, intended for the elevation and happiness of our race.

Beltenebrosa, going through the crucible of bodily pain, as she had already been proved in the furnace of mental affliction, realized the weakness of her sex and its insufficiency to stand alone. Knowing, at last, that she had found her master, she rejoiced to give him faithful service to her life's end. The wild nature was tamed; the hawk stooped to the lure; the gipsy became a meek and sincere Christian, a true, energetic, loving, and somewhat wilful wife.

But death had hovered all too near in that homely whitewashed room, and she herself hardly dared entertain a hope of recovery, resigned to the inevitable the more cheerfully that she had saved the man whose life she prized far above her own.

"My darling!" she murmured, pressing his hand to her lips, while her eyes wander from Matron to surgeon with the blank gaze of consciousness only half regained. "My darling, *you* are safe! that is enough. That is all I asked. I can die happy, and—and—" with a wan smile, "I don't care if Jericho got clear off with the money; he can't follow me where I am going now."

"Mr. Strange, control yourself," said the surgeon. "Be pleased to leave this lady exclusively to *me*. You shall go now, but may come again to-morrow at the same hour."

Then he fairly pushed him out of the room, but followed into the passage, where he whispered something that caused the curate's spirit to go up to heaven in a transport of gratitude, while tears no man need have been ashamed of relieved the tension of heart and brain.

"My own at last!" he repeated, talking wildly to himself as he walked home with swift, unequal strides. "My very own! I know it surely now. Life for life; what would a man have more? You bought mine at a fearful price, and yet, had you but known it, I have belonged to you for years."

How soon the mind jumps to conclusions! Passing a broker's shop, he found himself calculating the expenses of furnishing, and the articles necessary to a household with a lady at its head.

Like many excellent churchmen, he had considerably modified those ideas as to the celibacy of the clergy with which he entered on his ministry, and whereas he began by thinking the

priest should be hampered by no domestic affections, fettered by no earthly ties, he now arrived
at the conclusion that a man need serve Heaven
none the worse for those human interests and
responsibilities which enlarge his sympathies,
while they add to his experience, and that the
parson is only half a parson without a wife.

CHAPTER LX.

THE GAS TURNED OFF.

JUSTICE is represented in allegory as lame, blind-fold, and generally infirm; but we have the authority of Horace for insisting that even with a club-foot she seldom fails to overtake the *antecedentem scelestum*, the scoundrel who is making tracks to escape.

Jericho Lee, though he got off from his last outrage with better luck than he deserved, did not live to inflict further persecutions on his kinswoman, nor indeed to lay fresh contributions on the public. The failure of their joint attack caused much recrimination, and a permanent rupture between Zachary Cooper and himself.

Though he swore he would hang the tinker, Nance persuaded her husband that threatened men live long, and induced him to break off all connection with the profession by leaving Boars-haven surreptitiously, and travelling westward to the very brink of the Atlantic, where, amongst a primitive population descended from the Phœni-cians, bread might still be earned in the mend-ing of kettles, the tinkering of pots and pans. Jericho, vowing he was well rid of such a muff, undertook a burglary single-handed—playing it, he said, off his own bat, and this was the result.

He carefully reconnoitred a lone farmhouse, surrounded by wastes of moorland, with no cot-tage or other dwelling in sight or hearing. He ascertained that the farmer kept gold and silver for his men's weekly wages in a parlour on the ground floor; that he was in the habit of stay-ing out late of nights, particularly after market dinners, leaving only a feeble old woman and a herd-boy to guard the place. There seemed little risk attached to such a robbery as he planned, and Jericho laughed to think how contemptible was the danger in proportion to the spoil.

So about eleven o'clock on a moonless night he stole across the moor, crept under some outbuildings, and swinging himself on the ledge of the parlour window, proceeded to undo its fastenings from the outside with no little dexterity. He took pride in these niceties of his profession. An accomplished cracksman, he said, never blundered his work, and there was nothing so vulgar as noise !

He had lifted the sash, and was edging his body, feet foremost, into the room, when a powerful hand laid on his collar pulled him backwards to the ground, while a deep voice growled, with a wicked, half-triumphant chuckle, "I thowt as I shoold vind 'em at it ! I thowt as I shoold ! Ah ! do 'ee now ; do 'ee now, if ye dare ! "

The farmer, riding home from market, tolerably sober, and pacing through the bushy heather, that deadened his pony's footfall, growing, as it did, knee-high, turned the corner of his house so softly as to come upon the burglar in the act.

He was a strong, burly west-countryman, without an atom of fear in his composition, choleric withal, and one who dearly loved a tussle, either in sport or earnest. No wonder he had Jerry by the scruff of the neck and down on the heather ere a man could count ten.

The gipsy writhed in his grasp like an eel, but he was in a vice, and could not extricate himself; so he groped for his knife, and drew it, to urge the last desperate argument of crime! But he had an awkward customer to deal with,— skilled in wrestling, cudgel-play, all the ruder arts of self-defence. Flinging the other off as he would have wrung an adder from his sleeve, he leaped out of distance, and with his strong hammer-headed hunting-whip, delivered "one" that broke his antagonist's arm above the wrist, causing the knife to drop harmless from his hand. Then, taking wider scope and swing, he dealt another fatal blow that fairly cracked his adversary's skull.

Ere, with assistance of the startled inmates, he could carry Jericho into his house, the gipsy had been dead some minutes.

There was an inquest, of course, and the man-slayer gave his own version of the affair frankly enough. When asked if he had put all his strength into the *coup de grâce*, he replied, with rough simplicity, " I let 'un have it hard as ever I did know how ! Ev I'd only a-tickled 'un, a' was bound to scratch ! "

So Jericho Lee never wired a rabbit, picked a pocket, stabbed, blasphemed, nor came from his gipsy tents again, and extracted sovereigns from his kinswoman and Lord St. Moritz no more.

That nobleman, tired of gaiety, tired of society, tired of his ladyloves, tired, perhaps, chiefly of Lord St. Moritz himself, lounged over his *Morning Post* after breakfast, read in the same column the departure of Mrs. Stripwell for Italy, and the marriage of Beltenebrosa to Mervyn Strange, that dark and handsome widow being described in the peculiar phraseology affected by newspapers, as "Relict of the late James Paravant, Esq., of Combe-Wester and Appleton-Cleves."

The first piece of news affected him but little. Mrs. Stripwell and he were mutually bored with each other, and although he rather suspected the journey south was undertaken with the view of letting "poor Algy" down easy, to make room for a fresh admirer, he scarce gave the matter a thought. He was more concerned about "the relict of James Paravant, Esq.," and the certainty he now felt that she had never really cared for him in her heart—that he was no more to her than so many women had been to himself—a sop for vanity, the toy of an idle hour, an additional captive to swell the triumph, another flower to make up the garland—and that was all.

What a stupid paper! Not a word of news! Five columns devoted to a debate touching the " Law of Hypothec " in Scotland, on which, though only two understood it, every Scotch Member thought it right to have his say, reminding him of their countryman's definition of metaphysics : " When one man is explaining what he knows nothing about to another who cannot understand a word he says, that's 'meta-phœsics ! ' "

He lit a cigar. It didn't draw. Why was it impossible to get a good cigar in these days? He yawned, he stretched himself, he walked about the room, he stared through the windows at that most depressing of outlooks, an empty London street on a dull day, and found himself debarred even this melancholy consolation by the familiarity of a Savoyard with a hurdy-gurdy and a guinea-pig, who nodded and grinned at him as if they had robbed a church together the night before! There was nothing for it but to dress and go to his club.

When he got there it seemed gloomier than his own house. He had only taken his hat off once on his way, to salute Lady Goneril, who hurried by with averted head, nor showed the slightest intention of stopping her carriage to hold discourse. He could not tell—how should he?—that her Ladyship was making the best of her way home, with a swelled face, after a visit to the dentist for the stopping of her one unsound tooth! No; he thought she slighted him on purpose. She had other attractions now, younger, brighter, more notorious than himself; and this also was vanity!

A horrid suspicion shot across him! He must be growing old. Hang it, he must be *grown* old! In the morning-room of his club, two contemporaries, schoolfellows at Eton, sat reading the papers. One was as grey as a badger, the other had thrown out a portly stomach, and looked a hundred. Three or four young men came in like a whirlwind, he thought, as the young men nowadays *do* enter and leave a room. They were all talking at once, discussing some engrossing subject on which, to do them justice, they felt more sympathy than they showed. What was it?

" Had he not heard? Poor Beauregard died this morning. Six hours' illness. Three doctors called in—enough to kill any fellow! Poor Beau!" was their verdict. "What a good dinner he gave you! What good claret he had! What a good sportsman he was! After all, he was about due. He had a good long lease, and lived to a good old age!"

St. Moritz started, crossed the room, and looked in the *Peerage*. Yes, he thought so. Beauregard was exactly a month younger than himself. He had no heart to join in the conversation, but remained in his corner with the book open before him.

He gazed blankly round at the well-known chairs and tables, the clock that was never wrong, the familiar-looking glass that had reflected St. Moritz when he seldom required to shave. How long had he been a member of this very club? and what had he done with all the best years of a lifetime, no less irrecoverably gone, with their pleasures and their follies, than the bubbles we watch dancing down to destruction on a running stream? Like Byron's representative nobleman, he had " lived his life and gamed his gaming," the latter honestly enough; but as regarded the rest of the programme, had danced and voted but little, he thought, and shone not at all. Must he too remain " to be bored or bore?" The prospect was dreary in the extreme, and yet it seemed to close round him, narrowing every moment, thick and dull, like mist on an open moor.

Rousing himself from his abstraction, he looked about him as though waking out of a dream. The room was cleared. His two old cronies had departed, one to meet a soldier son from India, the other to take his grandchildren to the play. The young men had gone out as they came in, laughing, talking, and leaving the door open behind them. Lord St. Moritz was as much alone in this empty club as Robinson Crusoe in his island. Was he not also as much alone in the world? That world to which he had given his life, his energies, his affections, to find, now the gas had been turned off, it was but a theatre by daylight, after all. Glare, tinsel, and decorations had faded with the extinguished lamps. The hangings were but rags, the scenes tawdry; there was no background, the house was empty, and the stage was bare.

He went little to church, he read his Bible scarcely at all; yet the words of the Preacher came as forcibly to his mind as if they had been addressed to himself alone :

"Surely this also is vanity and vexation of spirit!"

THE END.

THOMAS CARLYLE'S WORKS.

LIBRARY EDITION COMPLETE.

Handsomely printed in 34 vols., demy 8vo, cloth.

SARTOR RESARTUS. The Life and Opinions of Herr Teufelsdrockh.
With a Portrait, 7s. 6d.

THE FRENCH REVOLUTION: A History. 3 vols., each 9s.

LIFE OF FREDERICK SCHILLER AND EXAMINATION OF
HIS WORKS. With Supplement of 1872, Portrait and Plates, 9s. The Supplement *separately*, 2s.

CRITICAL AND MISCELLANEOUS ESSAYS. With Portrait,
6 vols., each 9s.

ON HEROES, HERO WORSHIP, AND THE HEROIC IN
HISTORY. 7s. 6d.

PAST AND PRESENT. 9s.

OLIVER CROMWELL'S LETTERS AND SPEECHES. With
Portrait, 5 vols., each 9s.

LATTER-DAY PAMPHLETS. 9s.

LIFE OF JOHN STERLING. With Portraits, 9s.

HISTORY OF FREDERICK THE SECOND. 10 vols., each 9s.

TRANSLATIONS FROM THE GERMAN. 3 vols., each 9s.

GENERAL INDEX TO THE LIBRARY EDITION. 8vo, cloth,
6s.

MR. CARLYLE'S NEW WORK.

EARLY KINGS OF NORWAY; also AN ESSAY ON THE
PORTRAITS OF JOHN KNOX. Crown 8vo, with Portrait Illustrations,
7s. 6d.

CHEAP AND UNIFORM EDITION.

In 23 vols., crown 8vo, cloth.

THE FRENCH REVOLUTION. A
History. 2 vols., 12s.

OLIVER CROMWELL'S LETTERS
AND SPEECHES, with Elucidations, &c. 3 vols., 18s.

LIVES OF SCHILLER AND JOHN
STERLING. 1 vol., 6s.

CRITICAL AND MISCELLANEOUS
ESSAYS. 4 vols., £1 4s.

SARTOR RESARTUS AND LEC-
TURES ON HEROES. 1 vol., 6s.

LATTER-DAY PAMPHLETS. 1 vol.,
6s.

CHARTISM AND PAST AND PRE-
SENT. 1 vol., 6s.

TRANSLATIONS FROM THE GER-
MAN OF MUSÆUS, TIECK, AND
RICHTER. 1 vol., 6s.

WILHELM MEISTER, by Göethe, a
Translation. 2 vols., 12s.

HISTORY OF FRIEDRICH THE
SECOND. called Frederick the
Great. Vols. I. & II, containing
Part I.—"Friedrich till his Accession," 14s.—Vols. III. & IV., containing Part II.—"The First Two
Silesian Wars," 14s.—Vols. V., VI.,
VII., completing the Work, £1 1s.

PEOPLE'S EDITION.

37 Vols., small crown 8vo, price 2s. each vol., bound in cloth ; or in sets of 37 vols. in 18, cloth gilt, for £3 14s.

SARTOR RESARTUS.

FRENCH REVOLUTION   3 vols.

LIFE OF JOHN STERLING.

OLIVER CROMWELL'S LETTERS AND SPEECHES.   5 vols.

ON HEROES AND HERO WORSHIP.

PAST AND PRESENT.

CRITICAL AND MISCELLANEOUS ESSAYS.   7 vols.

LATTER-DAY PAMPHLETS.

LIFE OF SCHILLER.

FREDERICK THE GREAT.   10 vols.

WILHELM MEISTER.   3 vols.

TRANSLATIONS FROM MUSÆUS, TIECK, AND RICHTER. 2 vols.

THE EARLY KINGS OF NORWAY ; also AN ESSAY ON THE PORTRAITS OF JOHN KNOX.   With General Index.

WHYTE-MELVILLE'S WORKS.
CHEAP EDITION.

Crown 8vo, fancy boards, 2s. each, or 2s. 6d. in cloth.

UNCLE JOHN.   A NOVEL.

THE WHITE ROSE.

CERISE.   A TALE OF THE LAST CENTURY.

BROOKES OF BRIDLEMERE.

'BONES AND I;" 'OR, THE SKELETON AT HOME.

"M. OR N."   Similia Similibus Curantur.

CONTRABAND ; OR, A LOSING HAZARD.

MARKET HARBOROUGH ; OR, HOW MR. SAWYER WENT TO THE SHIRES.

SARCHEDON : A LEGEND OF THE GREAT QUEEN.

SONGS AND VERSES.

SATANELLA.   A STORY OF PUNCHESTOWN.

THE TRUE CROSS.   A LEGEND OF THE CHURCH.

KATERFELTO.   A STORY OF EXMOOR.

SISTER LOUISE ; or, A STORY OF A WOMAN'S REPENTANCE.

ROSINE.

THE WORKS OF CHARLES DICKENS.

THE ILLUSTRATED LIBRARY EDITION.

Complete in 30 volumes. Demy 8vo, 10s. each.

This edition is printed on a finer paper and in a larger type than has been employed in any previous edition. The type has been cast especially for it, and the page is of a size to admit of the introduction of all the original illustrations.

No such attractive issue has been made of the writings of Mr. Dickens, which, various as have been the forms of publication adapted to the demands of an ever widely increasing popularity. have never yet been worthily presented in a really handsome library form.

The collection comprises all the minor writings it was Mr. Dickens's wish to preserve.

SKETCHES BY BOZ. With 40 Illustrations by GEORGE CRUIKSHANK.

PICKWICK. 2 vols. With 42 Illustrations by " PHIZ."

OLIVER TWIST. With 24 Illustrations by CRUIKSHANK.

NICHOLAS NICKLEBY. 2 vols. With 40 Illustrations by " PHIZ."

OLD CURIOSITY SHOP *and* REPRINTED PIECES. 2 vols. With Illustrations by CATTERMOLE, &c.

BARNABY RUDGE *and* HARD TIMES. 2 vols. With Illustrations by CATTERMOLE, &c.

MARTIN CHUZZLEWIT. 2 vols. With 40 Illustrations by " PHIZ."

AMERICAN NOTES *and* PICTURES FROM ITALY. 1 vol. With 8 Illustrations.

DOMBEY AND SON. 2 vols. With 40 Illustrations by " PHIZ."

DAVID COPPERFIELD. 2 vols. With 40 Illustrations by " PHIZ."

BLEAK HOUSE. 2 vols. With 40 Illustrations by " PHIZ."

LITTLE DORRIT. 2 vols. With 40 Illustrations by " PHIZ."

A TALE OF TWO CITIES. With 16 Illustrations by " PHIZ."

THE UNCOMMERCIAL TRAVELLER. With 8 Illustrations by MARCUS STONE.

GREAT EXPECTATIONS. With 8 Illustrations by MARCUS STONE.

OUR MUTUAL FRIEND. 2 vols. With 40 Illustrations by MARCUS STONE.

CHRISTMAS BOOKS. With 17 Illustrations by SIR EDWIN LANDSEER, R.A., D. MACLISE, R.A., &c., &c.

HISTORY OF ENGLAND. With 8 Illustrations by MARCUS STONE.

CHRISTMAS STORIES (From " Household Words" and " All the Year Round.") With 14 Illustrations.

EDWIN DROOD AND OTHER STORIES. With 12 Illustrations by S. L. FILDES.

THE "CHARLES DICKENS" EDITION. In Crown 8vo.

In 21 vols. cloth, with Illustrations, £3 9s. Cd.

			£	s.	d.
PICKWICK PAPERS	With 8 Illustrations	...	0	3	6
MARTIN CHUZZLEWIT	With 8 ,,	...	0	3	6
DOMBEY AND SON	With 8 ,,	...	0	3	6
NICHOLAS NICKLEBY	With 8 ,,	...	0	3	6
DAVID COPPERFIELD	With 8 ,,	...	0	3	6
BLEAK HOUSE	With 8 ,,	...	0	3	6
LITTLE DORRIT	With 8 ,,	...	0	3	6
OUR MUTUAL FRIEND	With 8 ,,	...	0	3	6
BARNABY RUDGE	With 8 ,,	...	0	3	6
OLD CURIOSITY SHOP	With 8 ,,	...	0	3	6
A CHILD'S HISTORY OF ENGLAND	With 4 ,,	...	0	3	6
EDWIN DROOD *and* OTHER STORIES	With 8 ,,	...	0	3	6
CHRISTMAS STORIES FROM " HOUSEHOLD WORDS"	With 8 ,,	...	0	3	6
TALE OF TWO CITIES	With 8 ,,	...	0	3	0
SKETCHES BY BOZ	With 8 ,,	...	0	3	0
AMERICAN NOTES *and* REPRINTED PIECES	With 8 ,,	...	0	3	0
CHRISTMAS BOOKS	With 8 ,,	...	0	3	0
OLIVER TWIST	With 8 ,,	...	0	3	0
GREAT EXPECTATIONS	With 8 ,,	...	0	3	0
HARD TIMES *and* PICTURES FROM ITALY	With 8 ,,	...	0	3	0
UNCOMMERCIAL TRAVELLER	With 4 ,,	...	0	3	0

HOUSEHOLD EDITION.

In Crown 4to vols. Now Publishing, Sixpenny Monthly Parts.

19 Volumes completed.

OLIVER TWIST, with 28 Illustrations, cloth, 2s. 6d. ; paper, 1s. 9d.
MARTIN CHUZZLEWIT, with 59 Illustrations, cloth, 4s. ; paper, 3s.
DAVID COPPERFIELD, with 60 Illustrations and a Portrait, cloth, 4s. ; paper, 3s.
BLEAK HOUSE, with 61 Illustrations, cloth, 4s. ; paper, 3s.
LITTLE DORRIT, with 58 Illustrations, cloth, 4s. ; paper, 3s.
PICKWICK PAPERS, with 56 Illustrations, cloth, 4s. ; paper, 3s.
BARNABY RUDGE, with 46 Illustrations, cloth, 4s. ; paper, 3s.
A TALE OF TWO CITIES, with 25 Illustrations, cloth, 2s. 6d. ; paper, 1s. 9d.
OUR MUTUAL FRIEND, with 58 Illustrations, cloth, 4s. ; paper, 3s.
NICHOLAS NICKLEBY, with 59 Illustrations by F. Barnard. cloth, 4s. ; paper, 3s.
GREAT EXPECTATIONS, with 26 Illustrations by F. A. Fraser, cloth, 2s. 6d. ; paper,
1s. 9d.
OLD CURIOSITY SHOP, with 39 Illustrations by Charles Green, cloth, 4s. ; paper, 3s.
SKETCHES BY "BOZ," with 36 Illustrations by F. Barnard, cloth, 2s. 6d. ; paper, 1s.9d.
HARD TIMES, with 20 Illustrations by H. French, cloth, 2s. ; paper, 1s. 6d.
DOMBEY AND SON, with 61 Illustrations by F. Barnard, cloth, 4s. ; paper, 3s.
UNCOMMERCIAL TRAVELLER, with 26 Illustrations by E. G. Dalziel, cloth, 2s. 6d. ;
paper, 1s. 9d
CHRISTMAS BOOKS, cloth, 2s. 6d. ; sewed, 1s. 9d.
THE HISTORY OF ENGLAND, with 15 New Illustrations by J. M. C. RALSTON,
cloth, 2s. 6d. ; paper, 1s. 9d.
AMERICAN NOTES and PICTURES FROM ITALY, with 18 New Illustrations by
A. B. FROST and GORDON THOMSON. Cloth, 2s. 6d. ; paper, 1s. 9d,
The Volumes further to be published will consist of—
EDWIN DROOD ; STORIES ; and REPRINTED PIECES.
THE CHRISTMAS STORIES.
Besides the above will be included—
THE LIFE OF DICKENS. By JOHN FORSTER.

Messrs. CHAPMAN & HALL trust that by this Edition they will be enabled to place the works of the most popular British Author of the present day in the hands of all English readers.

193, PICCADILLY, LONDON, W.
DECEMBER, 1878.

Chapman and Hall's

CATALOGUE OF BOOKS.

INCLUDING

DRAWING EXAMPLES, DIAGRAMS, MODELS, INSTRUMENTS, ETC.

ISSUED UNDER THE AUTHORITY OF

THE SCIENCE AND ART DEPARTMENT, SOUTH KENSINGTON,

'OR THE USE OF SCHOOLS AND ART AND SCIENCE CLASSES.

NEW NOVELS.

WHYTE-MELVILLE.

BLACK BUT COMELY.

By MAJOR WHYTE-MELVILLE.

3 vols. *Early in January.*

ANTHONY TROLLOPE.

AN EYE FOR AN EYE.

By ANTHONY TROLLOPE.

2 vols. *Early in January.*

IN THIS WORLD.

By MABEL COLLINS.

2 vols.

YOUTH AT THE PROW.

By LADY WOOD.

3 vols. *In January.*

BLUE AND GREEN.

By SIR HENRY POTTINGER.

3 vols. *In January.*

CHAPMAN AND HALL'S ANNOUNCEMENTS.

December, 1878.

---

2 vols., demy 8vo, 32*s.*

The Public Life of the Earl of Beaconsfield.

BY FRANCIS HITCHMAN.

Demy 8vo.

IMPERIAL INDIA.

BY VAL PRINSEP.

ontaining Numerous Illustrations made during a Tour to the Courts of
the Principal Rajahs and Princes of India.

2 vols., demy 8vo, with Illustrations and Maps.

Sport in Burmah and Assam.

BY LIEUT.-COL. POLLOK.

With Notes of Sport in the Hilly Districts of the Northern Division,
Madras Presidency.

Large crown 8vo, 10*s.*

Pillars of the Empire.

WITH AN INTRODUCTION BY T. H. S. ESCOTT.

With Six Illustrations. Demy 8vo, 16*s.* Uniform with " On
the Frontier."

On Foot in Spain.

BY MAJOR CAMPION.

2 vols., large crown 8vo, 21*s.*

Shooting Adventures, Canine Lore, and Sea-Fishing Trips.

BY " WILDFOWLER," " SNAPSHOT."

Demy 8vo.

Memoirs of Sir Joshua Walmsley.

BY COLONEL WALMSLEY.

Illustrated. Demy 8vo, 6s.
Pretty Arts for the Employment of Leisure Hours.
By ELLIS A. DAVIDSON.

Small crown 8vo.
The Pleasures and Profits of Our Little Poultry Farm.
By MISS G. HILL.

New Volumes of the Library of Contemporary Science.
ESTHETICS. By EUGENE VÉRON.
PHILOSOPHY. Historical and Critical. By ANDRÉ LEFÈVRE.

South Kensington Art Handbooks.
New Vols. Illustrated.
SPANISH ART. By SENOR RIANO.
GLASS. By ALEXANDER NESBITT.

Large crown 8vo, with Portraits, 18s.
Hibernia Venatica.
By M. O'C. MORRIS, Author of "Triviata."

Large crown 8vo, 8s.
Autobiography of Sir G. Biddlecombe.
With a Portrait.

Foolscap 8vo, 6s.
BISMARCK'S LETTERS.
Translated by FITZᴴ MAXSE.

THE CHRONICLES OF BARSETSHIRE.
Messrs. CHAPMAN AND HALL
Also beg to announce the republication, in Monthly Volumes and under the above name, of the five following Novels by
MR. ANTHONY TROLLOPE :
THE WARDEN & BARCHESTER TOWERS.
2 vols. now ready.

DR. THORNE.
1 vol. ready.

FRAMLEY PARSONAGE.
1 vol.

THE LAST CHRONICLES OF BARSET.
2 vols.

Each Volume will contain a Frontispiece, and will be handsomely printed on large crown 8vo paper, 6s. each.

DICKENS'S WORKS.

Messrs. CHAPMAN AND HALL

BEG TO ANNOUNCE

A RE-ISSUE OF THE LIBRARY EDITION,

UNDER THE TITLE OF THE

POPULAR LIBRARY EDITION.

This Edition will be printed on good paper, and contain Illustrations that have appeared in the Household Edition, printed on plate paper.

Each Volume will consist of about 460 pages of Letterpress and

SIXTEEN ILLUSTRATIONS.

Large crown 8vo. Price 3s. 6d.

VOLUMES PUBLISHED.

"CHRISTMAS BOOKS."
"OLIVER TWIST."

BOOKS

PUBLISHED BY

CHAPMAN AND HALL.

ABBOTT (Edwin)—*Formerly Head-Master of the Philological School*—

A CONCORDANCE OF THE Original Poetical Works of Alexander Pope. With an Introduction on the English of Pope, by EDWIN A. ABBOTT, D.D. Medium 8vo, price £1 1s.

BARTLEY (G. C. T.)

A HANDY BOOK FOR GUARDians of the Poor : being a Complete Manual of the Duties of the Office, the Treatment of Typical Cases, with Practical Examples, etc. Crown 8vo, cloth, 3s.

THE PARISH NET : HOW IT'S Dragged and what it Catches. Crown 8vo, cloth, 7s. 6d.

THE SEVEN AGES OF A VILlage Pauper. Crown 8vo, cloth, 5s.

BEESLY (Edward Spencer), *Professor of History in University College, London.*

CATILINE, CLODIUS, AND Tiberius. Large Crown 8vo, 6s.

BENNETT (W. C.)

SEA SONGS. Crown 8vo, 4s.

BENSON (W.)

MANUAL OF THE SCIENCE of Colour. Coloured Frontispiece and Illustrations. 12mo, cloth, 2s. 6d.

PRINCIPLES OF THE SCIENCE of Colour. Small 4to, cloth, 15s.

BIDDLECOMBE (Sir Geo.) C.B., Captain R.N.

AUTOBIOGRAPHY OF SIR George Biddlecombe, C.B., Captain R.N. Large crown 8vo, with portrait, 8s.

BLAKE (Edith Osborne).

TWELVE MONTHS IN SOUTHern Europe. With Illustrations. Demy 8vo, 14s.

BLYTH (Colonel).

THE WHIST PLAYER. With Coloured Plates of "Hands." Third Edition. Imp. 16mo, cloth, 5s.

BRADLEY (Thomas), *of the Royal Military Academy, Woolwich.*

ELEMENTS OF GEOMETRIcal Drawing. In Two Parts, with Sixty Plates. Oblong-folio, halfbound, each Part 16s.

BUCKLAND (Frank).

LOG-BOOK OF A FISHERMAN and Zoologist. Second Edition. With numerous Illustrations. Large Crown 8vo, 12s.

BURCHETT (R.)

DEFINITIONS OF GEOMETRY. New Edition. 24mo, cloth, 5d.

LINEAR PERSPECTIVE, for the Use of Schools of Art. Twenty-first Thousand. With Illustrations. Post 8vo, cloth, 7s.

PRACTICAL GEOMETRY: The Course of Construction of Plane Geometrical Figures. With 137 Diagrams. Eighteenth Edition. Post 8vo, cloth, 5s.

CADDY (Mrs.)

HOUSEHOLD ORGANIZAtion. Crown 8vo, 4s.

CAMPION (J. S.), *late Major, Staff,* 1st Br. C.N.G., U.S.A.

ON THE FRONTIER. Reminiscences of Wild Sport, Personal Adventures, and Strange Scenes. With Illustrations. Demy 8vo. Second Edition, 16s.

ON FOOT IN SPAIN. With Illustrations. Demy 8vo, 16s.

CARLYLE (Dr.)

DANTE'S DIVINE COMEDY.— Literal Prose Translation of THE INFERNO, with Text and Notes. Second Edition. Post 8vo, 14s.

CLINTON (R. H.)

A COMPENDIUM OF ENGLISH HISTORY, from the Earliest Times to A.D. 1872. With Copious Quotations on the Leading Events and the Constitutional History, together with Appendices. Post 8vo, 7s. 6d.

CRAIK (George Lillie).

ENGLISH OF SHAKESPEARE. Illustrated in a Philological Commentary on his Julius Cæsar. Fifth Edition. Post 8vo, cloth, 5s.

OUTLINES OF THE HISTORY of The English Language. Ninth Edition. Post 8vo, cloth, 2s. 6d.

DASENT (Sir G. W.)

JEST AND EARNEST. A Collection of Reviews and Essays. 2 vols. Post 8vo, cloth, £1 1s.

TALES FROM THE FJELD. A Second Series of Popular Tales from the Norse of P. Ch. Asbjörnsen. Small 8vo, cloth, 10s. 6d.

DAUBOURG (E.)

INTERIOR ARCHITECTURE. Doors, Vestibules, Staircases, Anterooms, Drawing, Dining, and Bed Rooms, Libraries, Bank and Newspaper Offices, Shop Fronts and Interiors. With detailed Plans, Sections, and Elevations. A purely practical work, intended for Architects, Joiners, Cabinet Makers, Marble Workers, Decorators; as well as for the owners of houses who wish to have them ornamented by artisans of their own choice. Half-imperial, cloth, £2 12s. 6d.

DAVIDSON (Ellis A.)

PRETTY ARTS FOR THE EMployment of Leisure Hours. A Book for Ladies. With Illustrations. Demy 8vo, 6s.

THE AMATEUR HOUSE CARpenter: a Guide in Building, Making, and Repairing. With numerous Illustrations. Royal 8vo, 10s. 6d.

DAVISON (The Misses).

TRIQUETI MARBLES in the Albert Memorial Chapel, Windsor. A Series of Photographs. Dedicated by express permission to Her Majesty the Queen. The Work consists of 117 Photographs, with descriptive Letterpress, mounted on 49 sheets of cardboard, half imperial. Price £10 10s.

DE COIN (Col. Robert L.)

HISTORY AND CULTIVATION of Cotton and Tobacco. Post 8vo, cloth, 9s.

DE KONINCK (L. L.) and DIETZ (E.)

PRACTICAL MANUAL OF Chemical Assaying, as applied to the Manufacture of Iron from its Ores, and to Cast Iron, Wrought Iron, and Steel, as found in Commerce. Edited, with notes, by Robert Mallet. Post 8vo, cloth, 6s.

DE POMAR (The Duke).

FASHION AND PASSION ; or, Life in Mayfair. New Edition. Crown 8vo, 6s.

THE HEIR TO THE CROWN. Crown 8vo., 7s. 6d.

DYCE'S COLLECTION.

A CATALOGUE OF PRINTED Books and Manuscripts bequeathed by the Rev. Alexander Dyce to the South Kensington Museum. 2 vols. Royal 8vo, half-morocco, 14s.

A COLLECTION of PAINTINGS, Miniatures, Drawings, Engravings, Rings, and Miscellaneous Objects, bequeathed by the Rev. Alexander Dyce to the South Kensington Museum. Royal 8vo, half-morocco, 7s.

DIXON (W. Hepworth).

THE HOLY LAND. Fourth Edition. With 2 Steel and 12 Wood Engravings. Post 8vo, 10s. 6d.

DRAYSON (Lieut.-Col. A. W.)

THE CAUSE OF THE SUPposed Proper Motion of the Fixed Stars, with other Geometrical Problems in Astronomy hitherto unsolved. Demy 8vo, cloth, 10s.

THE CAUSE, DATE, AND Duration of the Last Glacial Epoch of Geology, with an Investigation of a New Movement of the Earth. Demy 8vo, cloth, 10s.

PRACTICAL MILITARY SURveying and Sketching. Fifth Edition. Post 8vo, cloth, 4s. 6d.

DYCE (William), R. A.

DRAWING-BOOK OF THE Government School of Design; or, Elementary Outlines of Ornament. Fifty selected Plates. Folio, sewed, 5s. ; mounted, 18s.

Text to Ditto. Sewed, 6d.

ELLIOT (Frances).

OLD COURT LIFE IN FRANCE. Third Edition. Demy 8vo, cloth, 10s. 6d.

THE DIARY OF AN IDLE Woman in Italy. Second Edition. Post 8vo, cloth, 6s.

PICTURES OF OLD ROME. New Edition. Post 8vo, cloth, 6s.

ENGEL (Carl).

A DESCRIPTIVE AND ILLUStrated Catalogue of the Musical Instruments in the South Kensington Museum, preceded by an Essay on the History of Musical Instruments. Second Edition. Royal 8vo, half-morocco. 12s.

ESCOTT (T. H. S.)

PILLARS OF THE EMPIRE: Short Biographical Sketches. Demy 8vo, 10s. 6d.

EWALD (Alexander Chas.) F.S.A.

THE LIFE AND TIMES OF Prince Charles Stuart. From the State Papers and other Sources. 2 vols. Demy 8vo, £1 8s.

SIR ROBERT WALPOLE. A Political Biography, 1676–1745. Demy 8vo, 18s.

FALLOUX (Count De), *of the French Academy.*

AUGUSTIN COCHIN. Translated from the French by Augustus Craven. Large crown 8vo, 9s.

FANE (Violet).

DENZIL PLACE: a Story in Verse. Crown 8vo, cloth, 8s.

QUEEN OF THE FAIRIES (A Village Story), and other Poems. Crown 8vo, 6s.

ANTHONY BABINGTON: a Drama Crown 8vo, 6s.

FLEMING (Geo.), F.R.C.S.

ANIMAL PLAGUES: THEIR History, Nature, and Prevention. 8vo, cloth, 15s.

HORSES AND HORSE-SHOE-ing: their Origin, History, Uses, and Abuses. 210 Engravings. 8vo, cloth, £1 1s.

PRACTICAL HORSE-SHOE-ing. With 37 Illustrations. Second Edition, enlarged. 8vo, sewed, 2s.

RABIES AND HYDROPHOBIA: Their History, Nature, Causes, Symptoms, and Prevention. With 8 Illustrations. 8vo, cloth, 15s.

FLEMING *(continued)*—

A MANUAL OF VETERINARY Sanitary Science and Police. With 33 Illustrations. 2 vols. Demy 8vo, 36s.

FORSTER (John).

THE LIFE OF CHARLES Dickens. Uniform with the "C. D." Edition of his Works. With numerous Illustrations. 2 vols. 7s.

THE LIFE OF CHARLES Dickens. With Portraits and other Illustrations. 15th Thousand. 3 vols. 8vo, cloth, £2 2s.

A New Edition in 2 vols. Demy 8vo, uniform with the Illustrated Edition Library of Dickens' Works. £1 8s.

SIR JOHN ELIOT: a Biography. With Portraits. New and cheaper Edition. 2 vols. Post 8vo, cloth, 14s.

OLIVER GOLDSMITH: a Biography. Small 8vo, cloth, 6s.

WALTER SAVAGE LANDOR: a Biography, 1775–1864. With Portraits and Vignettes. A New and Revised Edition, in 1 vol. Demy 8vo, 14s.

FORTNUM (C. D. E.)

A DESCRIPTIVE AND ILLUS-trated Catalogue of the Bronzes of European Origin in the South Kensington Museum, with an Introductory Notice. Royal 8vo, half-morocco, £1 10s.

A DESCRIPTIVE AND IL-lustrated Catalogue of Maiolica, Hispano-Moresco, Persian, Damascus, and Rhodian Wares in the South Kensington Museum. Royal 8vo, half-morocco, £2.

FRANCATELLI (C. E.)

ROYAL CONFECTIONER: English and Foreign. A Practical Treatise. With Coloured Illustrations. 3rd Edition. Post 8vo, cloth, 7s. 6d.

HALL (Sidney).

A TRAVELLING ATLAS OF the English Counties. Fifty Maps, coloured. New Edition, including the Railways, corrected up to the present date. Demy 8vo, in roan tuck, 10s. 6d.

HITCHMAN (Francis).

THE PUBLIC LIFE OF THE Earl of Beaconsfield. 2 vols. Demy 8vo, 32s.

HOLBEIN.

TWELVE HEADS AFTER HOLbein. Selected from Drawings in Her Majesty's Collection at Windsor. Reproduced in Autotype, in portfolio. 36s.

HOVELACQUE (Abel).

THE SCIENCE OF LANGUAGE: Linguistics, Philology, and Etymology. With Maps. Large crown 8vo, cloth, 5s.

HUMPHRIS (H. D.)

PRINCIPLES OF PERSPECtive. Illustrated in a Series of Examples. Oblong folio, halfbound, and Text 8vo, cloth, £1 1s.

JACQUEMART (Albert).

THE HISTORY OF FURNIture. Researches and Notes on Objects of Art which form Articles of Furniture, or would be interesting to Collectors. Edited by Mrs. Bury Palliser. With 200 Illustrations. Imperial 8vo. 31s. 6d.

JAGOR (F.)

PHILIPPINE ISLANDS, THE. With numerous Illustrations and a Map. Demy 8vo, 16).

JARRY (General).

NAPIER (MAJ.-GEN. W. C. E.) Outpost Duty. Translated, with Treatises on Military Reconnaissance and on Road-Making. Third Edition. Crown 8vo, 5s.

KELLEY, M.D. (E.G.)

THE PHILOSOPHY OF EXistence. The Reality and Romance of Histories. Demy 8vo, 16s.

KEMPIS (Thomas A.)

OF THE IMITATION OF CHRIST. Four Books. Beautifully Illustrated Edition. Demy 8vo, 16s.

KLACZKO (M. Julian).

TWO CHANCELLORS: Prince Gortschakof and Prince Bismarck. Translated by Mrs. Tait. New and cheaper edition, 6s.

LEFEVRE (Andre).

PHILOSOPHY, Historical and Critical. [In the Press.

LENNOX (Lord William).

FASHION THEN AND NOW. 2 vols. Demy 8vo, 28s.

LETOURNEAU (Dr. Charles).

BIOLOGY. With Illustrations. Large crown 8vo. 6s.

LUCAS (Captain).

CAMP LIFE AND SPORT IN South Africa. With Episodes in Kaffir Warfare. With Illustrations. Demy 8vo, 12s.

LYTTON (Robert Lord).

POETICAL WORKS, collected edition. Complete in 5 vols.
Fables in Song. 2 vols. Fcap. 8vo, 12s.
Lucile. Fcap. 8vo, 6s.
The Wanderer. Fcap. 8vo. 6s.
Poems, Historical and Characteristic. Fcap. 6s.

MALLET (Dr. J. W.)

COTTON : THE CHEMICAL, etc., conditions of its successful cultivation. Post 8vo, cloth, 7s. 6d.

MALLET (Robert).

GREAT NEAPOLITAN Earthquake of 1857. Maps and numerous Illustrations. 2 vols. Royal 8vo, cloth, £3 3s.

MASKELL (William).

A DESCRIPTION OF THE Ivories, Ancient and Mediæval, in the South Kensington Museum, with a Preface. With numerous Photographs and Woodcuts. Royal 8vo. half morocco, £1 1s.

MAXSE (Fitzh.)

PRINCE BISMARCK'S Letters. Translated from the German. Small crown 8vo, cloth 6s. Second Edition.

MAZADE (Charles De).

THE LIFE OF COUNT Cavour. Translated from the French. Demy 8vo, 16s.

MELVILLE (G. J. Whyte).

RIDING RECOLLECTIONS. With Illustrations by Edgar Giberne. Large crown 8vo. Sixth Edition. 12s.

MELVILLE (*continued*)—

ROY'S WIFE. By G. J. Whyte-Melville. New and Cheaper Edition, 6s.

ROSINE. With Illustrations. Demy 8vo. Uniform with "Katerfelto," 16s.

SISTER LOUISE : With illustrations. Demy 8vo, 16s.

KATERFELTO : A Story of Exmoor. With 12 Illustrations by Colonel H. Hope Crealocke, Fourth Edition. Large crown, 8s.

CHEAP EDITION.

Crown 8vo, fancy boards, 2s. each, or 2s. 6d. in cloth.

UNCLE JOHN.

THE WHITE ROSE.

CERISE.

BROOKES OF BRIDLEMERE.

"BONES AND I ; "

"M., OR N."

CONTRABAND ;

MARKET HARBOROUGH;

SARCHEDON.

SONGS AND VERSES.

SATANELLA.

THE TRUE CROSS. A Legend of the Church.

KATERFELTO.

SISTER LOUISE.

ROSINE.

MEREDITH (George).

MODERN LOVE, AND POEMS of the English Roadside, with Poems and Ballads. Fcap. 8vo, cloth, 6s.

MOLESWORTH (W. Nassau).

HISTORY OF ENGLAND from the year 1830 to the Resignation of the Gladstone Ministry.

A Cheap Edition, carefully revised, and carried up to March, 1874. 3 vols. crown 8vo, 18s.

A School Edition. Post 8vo, 7s. 6d.

MORLEY (Henry).

ENGLISH WRITERS. Vol. I. Part I. The Celts and Anglo-Saxons. With an Introductory Sketch of the Four Periods of English Literature. Part II. FROM THE CONQUEST TO CHAUCER. (Making 2 vols.), 8vo, cloth, £1 2s.

. Each Part is indexed separately. The Two Parts complete the account of English literature during the Period of the Formation of the language, or of THE WRITERS BEFORE CHAUCER.

Vol. II. Part I. FROM CHAUCER to Dunbar. 8vo, cloth, 12s.

TABLES OF ENGLISH LITE-rature. Containing 20 Charts. Second Edition, with Index. Royal 4to, cloth, 12s.

MORLEY (John).

DIDEROT AND THE ENCY-clopædists. 2 vols., demy 8vo, 26s.

CRITICAL MISCELLANIES. Second Series.

VOLTAIRE Large crown 8vo, 6s.

ROUSSEAU. Large crown 8vo, 9s.

CRITICAL MISCELLANIES. First Series. Large crown 8vo, 6s.

CRITICAL MISCELLANIES. Second Series. In the Press.

MORLEY, J. (*continued*)—

ON COMPROMISE. New Edition. Crown 8vo, 3s. 6d.

STRUGGLE FOR NATIONAL Education. Third Edition. 8vo, cloth, 3s.

MORRIS (M. O'Connor).

HIBERNICA VENATICA. With Portraits of the Marchioness of Waterford, the Marchioness of Ormonde, Lady Randolph Churchill, Hon. Mrs. Malone, Miss Persse (of Moyode Castle), Mrs. Stewart Duckett, and Miss Myra Watson. Large crown 8vo, 18s.

TRIVIATA; or, Cross Road Chronicles of Passages in Irish Hunting History during the season of 1875-6. With Illustrations. Large crown 8vo, 16s.

NEWTON (E. Tulley, F.G.S.) *Assistant Naturalist H.M. Geological Survey.*

THE TYPICAL PARTS IN THE Skeletons of a Cat, Duck, and Codfish, being a Catalogue with Comparative Descriptions arranged in a Tabular Form. Demy 8vo, cloth, 3s.

O'CONNELL (Mrs. Morgan JOHN).

CHARLES BIANCONI. a Biography. 1786-1875. By his Daughter. With Illustrations. Demy 8vo, 10s. 6d.

OLIVER (Prof.), F.R.S. &c.

ILLUSTRATIONS of the PRIN-cipal Natural Orders of the Vegetable Kingdom, Prepared for the Science and Art Department, South Kensington. Oblong 8vo, with 109 Plates. Price, plain, 16s.; coloured, £1 6s.

OZANE (I. W.)

THREE YEARS in ROUMANIA. Large crown 8vo, 7s. 6d.

PIERCE (Gilbert A.)

THE DICKENS DICTIONARY: a Key to the Characters and Principal Incidents in the Tales of Charles Dickens. With Additions by William A. Wheeler. Large crown 8vo, 10s. 6d.

POLLEN (J. H.)

ANCIENT and MODERN FURniture and Woodwork in the South Kensington Museum. With an Introduction, and Illustrated with numerous Coloured Photographs and Woodcuts. Royal 8vo, half-morocco, £1 1s.

PUCKETT (R. Campbell), *Head-Master of the Bath School of Art.*

SCIOGRAPHY; or, Radical Projection of Shadows. New Edition. Crown 8vo, cloth, 6s.

RANKEN (W. H. L.)

THE DOMINION OF AUSTRAlia. An Account of its Foundations. Post 8vo, cloth, 12s.

REDGRAVE (Richard).

MANUAL AND CATECHISM on Colour. 24mo, cloth, 9d.

REDGRAVE (Samuel).

A DESCRIPTIVE CATALOGUE of the Historical Collection of Water-Colour Paintings in the South Kensington Museum. With an Introductory Notice by Samuel Redgrave. With numerous Chromo-lithographs and other Illustrations. Published for the Science and Art Department of the Committee of Council on Education. Royal 8vo, £1 1s.

RIDGE (Dr. Benjamin).

OURSELVES, OUR FOOD, and Our Physic. Twelfth Edition. Fcap. 8vo, cloth, 1s. 6d.

ROBINSON (C. E.)

THE CRUISE of the WIDGEON; 700 Miles in a Ten-Ton Yawl. Second Edition. Large crown 8vo, 9s.

ROBINSON (J. C.)

ITALIAN SCULPTURE of the Middle Ages and Period of the Revival of Art. With 20 Engravings. Royal 8vo, cloth, 7s. 6d.

ROBSON (George).

ELEMENTARY BUILDING Construction. Illustrated by a Design for an Entrance, Lodge, and Gate. 15 Plates, Oblong folio, sewed, 8s.

ROBSON (Rev. J. H., M.A., LL.M.), *Late Foundation Scholar of Downing College, Cambridge.*

AN ELEMENTARY TREATISE on Algebra. Post 8vo, 6s.

ROCK (The Rev. Canon, D.D.)

ON TEXTILE FABRICS. A Descriptive and Illustrated Catalogue of the Collection of Church Vestments, Dresses, Silk Stuffs, Needlework, and Tapestries in the South Kensington Museum. Roy. 8vo, half-mor., £1 11s. 6d.

SALUSBURY (Philip E. B.), *Lieut. 1st Royal Cheshire Light Infantry.*

TWO MONTHS WITH TCHERnaieff in Servia. Large crown 8vo, 9s.

SHIRREFF (Emily).

A SKETCH OF THE LIFE OF Friedrich Fröbel, together with a Notice of Madame von Marenholtz Bulow's Personal Recollections of F. Fröbel. Crown 8vo, sewn, 1s.

SKERTCHLY (J. A.)

DAHOMEY AS IT IS: being a Narrative of Eight Months' Residence in that Country, with a Full Account of the Notorious Annual Customs, and the Social and Religious Institutions of the Ffons. With Illustrations. 8vo, cloth, £1 1s.

SMITHARD   (Marian), *First-class Diplomée from National Training School, South Kensington.*

COOKERY FOR THE ARTISAN and others: being a selection of over two hundred Useful Receipts. Sewed, 1s.

SPALDING (Captain).

KHIVA AND TURKESTAN, translated from the Russian, with Map. Large crown 8vo, 9s.

ST. CLAIR (S. G. B.), *Captain late 21st Fusiliers.*

TWELVE YEARS' RESIDENCE in Bulgaria. Revised Edition. Demy 8vo, 9s.

STORY (W. W.)

ROBA DI ROMA. Seventh Edition, with Additions and Portrait. Post 8vo, cloth, 10s. 6d.

THE PROPORTIONS OF THE Human Frame, according to a New Canon. With Plates. Royal 8vo, 10s.

STORY (*continued*)—

CASTLE ST. ANGELO. Uniform with "Roba di Roma." With Illustrations. Large crown 8vo, 10s. 6d.

STREETER (E. W.)

PRECIOUS STONES AND Gems. An exhaustive and practical Work for the Merchant-Connoisseur, or the Private Buyer With coloured Illustrations, Photographs, etc. Demy 8vo, 18s.

GOLD; OR, LEGAL REGUlations for this Metal in different Countries of the World. Crown 8vo, cloth, 3s. 6d.

TOPINARD (Dr. Paul).

ANTHROPOLOGY. With a Preface by Professor Paul Broca. With numerous Illustrations. Large crown 8vo, 7s. 6d.

TROLLOPE (Anthony).

THE CHRONICLES OF BARsetshire. A uniform Edition in the Press, consisting of 6 vols., large crown 8vo, handsomely printed.

> THE WARDEN.
> BARCHESTER TOWERS.
> DR. THORNE.
> FRAMLEY PARSONAGE.
> LAST CHRONICLE OF
>   BARSET. 2 vols.

Large crown 8vo, each vol. containing Frontispiece. Vol. 2 now ready.

AUSTRALIA AND NEW ZEALAND. A cheap Edition in four parts, with Maps. Small 8vo, cloth, 3s. each.

> NEW ZEALAND.
> VICTORIA AND TASMANIA.
> NEW SOUTH WALES AND
>   QUEENSLAND..
> SOUTH AUSTRALIA AND WESTERN AUSTRALIA.

TROLLOPE (*continued*)—

SOUTH AFRICA. 2 vols. Large crown 8vo, with Maps. Fourth Edition. £1 10s.

WAHL (O. H.)

THE LAND OF THE CZAR. Demy 8vo, 16s.

WESTWOOD (J. O.), M.A., F.L.S., etc. etc.

A DESCRIPTIVE AND ILLUStrated Catalogue of the Fictile Ivories in the South Kensington Museum. With an Account of the Continental Collections of Classical and Mediæval Ivories. Royal 8vo, half-morocco, £1 4s.

WHEELER (G. P.)

VISIT OF THE PRINCE OF Wales. A Chronicle of H.R.H.'s Journeyings in India, Ceylon, Spain, and Portugal. Large crown 8vo, 12s.

WHITE (Walter).

HOLIDAYS IN TYROL: Kufstein, Klobenstein, and Paneveggio. Large crown 8vo, 14s.

EASTERN ENGLAND. From the Thames to the Humber. 2 vols. Post 8vo, cloth, 18s.

MONTH IN YORKSHIRE. Fourth Edition. With a Map. Post 8vo, cloth, 4s.

LONDONER'S WALK TO THE Land's End, and a Trip to the Scilly Isles. With 4 Maps. Second Edition. Post 8vo, 4s.

WORNUM (R. N.)

HOLBEIN (HANS)—LIFE. With Portrait and Illustrations. Imperial 8vo, cloth, £1 11s. 6d.

WORNUM (*continued*)—

ANALYSIS OF ORNAMENT: The Characteristics of Styles. An Introduction to the Study of the History of Ornamental Art. With many Illustrations. Sixth Edition. Royal 8vo, cloth, 8s.

WYON (F. W.)

HISTORY OF GREAT BRITAIN during the reign of Queen Anne. 2 vols. Demy 8vo, £1 12s.

YOUNGE (C. D.)

PARALLEL LIVES OF ANcient and Modern Heroes. New Edition. 12mo, cloth, 4s. 6d.

CEYLON: being a General Description of the Island, Historical, Physical, Statistical. Containing the most Recent Information. With Map. By an Officer, late of the Ceylon Rifles. 2 vols. Demy 8vo, £1 8s.

COLONIAL EXPERIENCES; or, Incidents and Reminiscences of Thirty-four Years in New Zealand. By an Old Colonist. With a Map. Crown 8vo, 8s.

ELEMENTARY DRAWINGBook. Directions for Introducing the First Steps of Elementary Drawing in Schools and among Workmen. Small 4to, cloth, 4s. 6d.

FORTNIGHTLY REVIEW— First Series, May, 1865; to Dec. 1866. 6 vols. Cloth, 13s. each.

New Series, 1867 to 1872. In Half-yearly Volumes. Cloth, 13s. each.

From January, 1873, to June, 1878, in Half-yearly Volumes. Cloth, 16s. each.

NATIONAL TRAINING School for Cookery. Containing Lessons on Cookery; forming the Course of Instruction in the School. With List of Utensils Necessary, and Lessons on Cleaning Utensils. Compiled by "R. O. C." Large crown 8vo. Third Edition, 8s.

PAST DAYS IN INDIA ; or, Sporting Reminiscences of the Valley of the Saone and the Basin of Singrowree. By a late Customs Officer, N.W. Provinces, India. Post 8vo, 10s. 6d.

SHOOTING AND FISHING Trips in England, France, Alsace, Belgium, Holland, and Bavaria. By "Wildfowler," "Snapshot." New Edition, with Illustrations. Large crown 8vo, 8s.

HOME LIFE. A Handbook and Elementary Instruction, containing Practical Suggestions addressed to Managers and Teachers of Schools, intended to show how the underlying principles of Home Duties or Domestic Economy may be the basis of National Primary Instruction. Crown 8vo, 3s.

SHOOTING, YACHTING, AND Sea-Fishing Trips, at Home and on the Continent. Second Series. By "Wildfowler," "Snapshot." 2. vols. Crown 8vo, £1 1s.

UNIVERSAL CATALOGUE OF Books on Art. Compiled for the use of the National Art Library, and the Schools of Art in the United Kingdom. In 2 vols. Crown 4to, half-morocco, £2 2s.

SOUTH KENSINGTON MUSEUM SCIENCE AND ART HANDBOOKS.

Published for the Committee of Council on Education.

TAPESTRY. By Alfred Champeaux. With Woodcuts, 2s. 6d.

BRONZES. By C. Drury E. Fortnum, F.S.A. With numerous Woodcuts. Large crown 8vo, 2s. 6d.

ANIMAL PRODUCTS: their Preparation, Commercial Uses, and Value. By T. L. Simmonds, Editor of the *Journal of Applied Science*. Large crown 8vo, 7s. 6d.

FOOD: A Short Account of the Sources, Constituents, and Uses of Food; intended chiefly as a Guide to the Food Collection in the Bethnal Green Museum. By A. H. Church, M.A., Oxon., Professor of Chemistry in the Agricultural College, Cirencester. Large crown 8vo, 3s.

PLAIN WORDS ABOUT Water. By A. H. Church, M.A., Oxon., Professor of Chemistry in the Agricultural College, Cirencester. Large crown 8vo, sewed, 6d.

SCIENCE CONFERENCES. Delivered at the South Kensington Museum. Crown 8vo, 2 vols., 6s. each.

Vol. I.—Physics and Mechanics. Vol. II. — Chemistry, Biology, Physical Geography, Geology, Mineralogy, and Meteorology.

HANDBOOK TO THE SPECIAL Loan Collection of Scientific Apparatus. Large crown 8vo, 3s.

THE INDUSTRIAL ARTS: Historical Sketches. With 242 Illustrations. Demy 8vo, 7s. 6d.

ECONOMIC ENTOMOLOGY. By Andrew Murray, F.L.S., APTERA. With numerous Illustrations. Large crown 8vo, 7s. 6d.

TEXTILE FABRICS. By the Very Rev. Daniel Rock, D.D. With numerous Woodcuts. Large crown 8vo, 2s. 6d.

IVORIES: ANCIENT AND Mediæval. By William Maskell. With numerous Woodcuts. Large crown 8vo, 2s. 6d.

ANCIENT AND MODERN FURniture and Woodwork. By John Hungerford Pollen. With numerous Woodcuts. Large crown 8vo, 2s. 6d.

PERSIAN ART. By Major R. Murdock Smith, R.E. With Additional Illustrations. [*In the press.*]

MAIOLICA. By C. Drury, E. Fortnum, F.S.A. With numerous Woodcuts. Large crown 8vo, 2s. 6d.

MUSICAL INSTRUMENTS. By Carl Engel. With numerous Woodcuts. Large crown 8vo, 2s. 6d.

MANUAL OF DESIGN, compiled from the Writings and Addresses of Richard Redgrave, R.A. By Gilbert R. Redgrave. With Woodcuts. Large crown 8vo, 2s. 6d.

FREE EVENING LECTURES. Delivered in connection with the Special Loan Collection of Scientific Apparatus, 1876. Large crown 8vo, 8s.

CARLYLE'S (THOMAS) WORKS.
LIBRARY EDITION COMPLETE.
Handsomely Printed in 34 *vols. Demy* 8vo, *cloth,* £15.

SARTOR RESARTUS. The Life and Opinions of Herr Teufelsdröck. With a Portrait, 7s. 6d.

THE FRENCH REVOLUTION. A History. 3 vols., each 9s.

LIFE OF FREDERICK SCHILler and Examination of his Works. With Supplement of 1872. Portrait and Plates, 9s. The Supplement *separately*, 2s.

CRITICAL AND MISCELLAneous Essays. With Portrait. 6 vols., each 9s.

ON HEROES, HERO WORSHIP, and the Heroic in History. 7s. 6d.

PAST AND PRESENT. 9s.

OLIVER CROMWELL'S LETters and Speeches. With Portraits. 5 vols., each 9s.

LATTER-DAY PAMPHLETS. 9s.

LIFE OF JOHN STERLING. With Portrait, 9s.

HISTORY OF FREDERICK the Second. 10 vols., each 9s.

TRANSLATIONS FROM THE German. 3 vols,, each 9s.

GENERAL INDEX TO THE Library Edition. 8vo, cloth, 6s.

CHEAP AND UNIFORM EDITION.

In 23 vols. Crown 8vo, cloth, £7 5s.

THE FRENCH REVOLUTION:
A History. 2 vols., 12s.

OLIVER CROMWELL'S LET-
ters and Speeches, with Elucidations, &c. 3 vols., 18s.

LIVES OF SCHILLER AND
John Sterling. 1 vol., 6s.

CRITICAL AND MISCELLA-
neous Essays. 4 vols., £1 4s.

SARTOR RESARTUS AND LEC-
tures on Heroes. 1 vol., 6s.

LATTER-DAY   PAMPHLETS.
1 vol., 6s.

CHARTISM AND PAST AND
Present. 1 vol., 6s.

TRANSLATIONS FROM THE
German of Musæus, Tieck, and
Richter. 1 vol., 6s.

WILHELM MEISTER, by Göthe.
A Translation. 2 vols., 12s.

HISTORY OF FRIEDRICH THE
Second, called Frederick the
Great, 14s. Vols. V., VI., VII.,
completing the Work, £1 1s.
7 Vols. 49s.

PEOPLE'S EDITION.

*In 37 vols., small Crown 8vo. Price 2s. each vol. bound in cloth, or in sets
of 37 vols. in 18, cloth gilt, for £3 14s.*

SARTOR RESARTUS.

FRENCH REVOLUTION. 3 vols.

LIFE OF JOHN STERLING.

OLIVER CROMWELL'S LET-
ters and Speeches. 5 vols.

ON HEROES AND HERO
WORSHIP.

PAST AND PRESENT.

CRITICAL AND MISCELLA-
neous Essays. 7 vols.

LATTER-DAY PAMPHLETS.

LIFE OF SCHILLER.

FREDERICK THE GREAT. 10
vols.

WILHELM MEISTER, 3 vols.

TRANSLATIONS FROM MU-
sæus, Tieck, and Richter. 2 vols.

THE EARLY KINGS OF NOR-
way; also an Essay on the Portraits of John Knox, with Illustrations.

DICKENS'S (CHARLES) WORKS.

ORIGINAL EDITIONS.

In Demy 8vo.

THE MYSTERY OF EDWIN DROOD. With Illustrations by S. L. Fildes, and a Portrait engraved by Baker. Cloth, 7s. 6d.

OUR MUTUAL FRIEND. With Forty Illustrations by Marcus Stone. Cloth, £1 1s.

THE PICKWICK PAPERS. With Forty-three Illustrations by Seymour and Phiz. Cloth, £1 1s.

NICHOLAS NICKLEBY. With Forty Illustrations by Phiz. Cloth, £1 1s.

SKETCHES BY "BOZ." With Forty Illustrations by George Cruikshank. Cloth, £1 1s.

MARTIN CHUZZLEWIT. With Forty Illustrations by Phiz. Cloth, £1 1s.

DOMBEY AND SON. With Forty Illustrations by Phiz. Cloth, £1 1s.

DAVID COPPERFIELD. With Forty Illustrations by Phiz. Cloth, £1 1s.

BLEAK HOUSE. With Forty Illustrations by Phiz. Cloth, £1 1s.

LITTLE DORRIT. With Forty Illustrations by Phiz. Cloth, £1 1s.

THE OLD CURIOSITY SHOP. With Seventy-five Illustrations by George Cattermole and H. K. Browne. A New Edition. Uniform with the other volumes, £1 1s.

BARNABY RUDGE : a Tale of the Riots of 'Eighty. With Seventy-eight Illustrations by G. Cattermole and H. K. Browne. Uniform with the other volumes, £1 1s.

CHRISTMAS BOOKS : Containing — The Christmas Carol ; The Cricket on The Hearth ; The Chimes ; The Battle of Life ; The Haunted House. With all the original Illustrations. Cloth, 12s.

OLIVER TWIST AND TALE OF TWO CITIES. In one volume. Cloth, £1 1s.

OLIVER TWIST. Separately. With Twenty-four Illustrations by George Cruikshank.

A TALE OF TWO CITIES. Separately. With Sixteen Illustrations by Phiz. Cloth, 9s.

*** *The remainder of Dickens's Works were not originally printed in Demy 8vo.*

LIBRARY EDITION.

In Post 8vo. With the Original Illustrations, 30 Vols., Cloth, £12.

				s.	d.
PICKWICK PAPERS	. 43 Illustrations,	2 vols.	16	0
NICHOLAS NICKLEBY	. 39	,,	2 vols.	16	0
MARTIN CHUZZLEWIT	. 40	,,	2 vols.	16	0
OLD CURIOSITY SHOP and REPRINTED PIECES	. 36	,,	2 vols.	16	0
BARNABY RUDGE and HARD TIMES	. 36	,,	2 vols.	16	0
BLEAK HOUSE	. 40	,,	2 vols.	16	0
LITTLE DORRIT	. 40	,,	2 vols.	16	0
DOMBEY AND SON	. 38	,,	2 vols.	16	0
DAVID COPPERFIELD	. 38	,,	2 vols.	16	0
OUR MUTUAL FRIEND	. 40	,,	2 vols.	16	0
SKETCHES BY "BOZ"	. 39	,,	1 vol.	8	0
OLIVER TWIST	. 24	,,	1 vol.	8	0
CHRISTMAS BOOKS	. 17	,,	1 vol.	8	0
A TALE OF TWO CITIES	. 16	,,	1 vol.	8	0
GREAT EXPECTATIONS	. 8	,,	1 vol.	8	0
PICTURES FROM ITALY and AMERICAN NOTES	. 8	,,	1 vol.	8	0
UNCOMMERCIAL TRAVELLER	. 8	,,	1 vol.	8	0
CHILD'S HISTORY OF ENGLAND	. 8	,,	1 vol.	8	0
EDWIN DROOD and MISCELLANIES	. 12	,,	1 vol.	8	0
CHRISTMAS STORIES from "Household Words," etc.	. 14	,,	1 vol.	8	0

THE LIFE OF CHARLES DICKENS. By JOHN FORSTER. A New Edition. With Illustrations. Uniform with this Edition, post 8vo, of his Works. In one vol. 10s. 6d.

THE "CHARLES DICKENS" EDITION.

In Crown 8vo. In 21 vols., cloth, with Illustrations, £3 9s. 6d.

				s.	d.
PICKWICK PAPERS	.	8 Illustrations	3	6
MARTIN CHUZZLEWIT	.	8	,,	3	6
DOMBEY AND SON	.	8	,,	3	6
NICHOLAS NICKLEBY	.	8	,,	3	6
DAVID COPPERFIELD	.	8	,,	3	6
BLEAK HOUSE	.	8	,,	3	6
LITTLE DORRIT	.	8	,,	3	6
OUR MUTUAL FRIEND	.	8	,,	3	6
BARNABY RUDGE	.	8	,,	3	6
OLD CURIOSITY SHOP	.	8	,,	3	6
A CHILD'S HISTORY OF ENGLAND	.	4	,,	3	6
EDWIN DROOD AND OTHER STORIES	.	8	,,	3	6
CHRISTMAS STORIES, from "Household Words"	8	,,	3	0
TALE OF TWO CITIES	.	8	,,	3	0
SKETCHES BY "BOZ"	.	8	,,	3	0
AMERICAN NOTES and REPRINTED PIECES	.	8	,,	3	0
CHRISTMAS BOOKS	.	8	,,	3	0
OLIVER TWIST	.	8	,,	3	0
GREAT EXPECTATIONS	.	8	,,	3	0
HARD TIMES and PICTURES FROM ITALY	.	8	,,	3	0
UNCOMMERCIAL TRAVELLER	.	4	,,	3	0

THE LIFE OF CHARLES DICKENS. Uniform with this Edition, with Numerous Illustrations. 2 vols. 3s. 6d. each.

THE ILLUSTRATED LIBRARY EDITION.

Complete in 30 Volumes. Demy 8vo, 10s. *each ; or set,* £15.

This Edition is printed on a finer paper and in a larger type than has been employed in any previous edition. The type has been cast especially for it, and the page is of a size to admit of the introduction of all the original illustrations.

No such attractive issue has been made of the writings of Mr. Dickens, which, various as have been the forms of publication adapted to the demands of an ever widely-increasing popularity, have never yet been worthily presented in a really handome library form.

The collection comprises all the minor writings it was Mr. Dickens's wish to preserve.

SKETCHES BY " BOZ." With 40 Illustrations by G. Cruikshank.

PICKWICK PAPERS. 2 vols. With 42 Illustrations by Phiz.

OLIVER TWIST. With 24 Illustrations by Cruikshank.

NICHOLAS NICKLEBY. 2 vols. With 40 Illustrations by Phiz.

OLD CURIOSITY SHOP and REPRINTED PIECES. 2 vols. With Illustrations by Cattermole, etc.

BARNABY RUDGE and HARD TIMES, 2 vols. With Illustrations by Cattermole, etc.

MARTIN CHUZZLEWIT. 2 vols. With 40 Illustrations by Phiz.

AMERICAN NOTES and PICTURES FROM ITALY. 1 vol. With 8 Illustrations.

DOMBEY AND SON. 2 vols. With 40 Illustrations by Phiz.

DAVID COPPERFIELD. 2 vols. With 40 Illustrations by Phiz.

BLEAK HOUSE. 2 vols. With 40 Illustrations by Phiz.

LITTLE DORRIT. 2 vols. With 40 Illustrations by Phiz.

A TALE OF TWO CITIES. With 16 Illustrations by Phiz.

THE UNCOMMERCIAL TRAVELLER. With 8 Illustrations by Marcus Stone.

GREAT EXPECTATIONS. With 8 Illustrations by Marcus Stone.

OUR MUTUAL FRIEND. 2 vols. With 40 Illustrations by Marcus Stone.

CHRISTMAS BOOKS. With 17 Illustrations by Sir Edwin Landseer, R.A., Maclise, R.A., etc. etc.

HISTORY OF ENGLAND. With 8 Illustrations by Marcus Stone.

CHRISTMAS STORIES. (From "Household Words" and "All the Year Round.") With 14 Illustrations.

EDWIN DROOD AND OTHER STORIES. With 12 Illustrations by S. L. Fildes.

HOUSEHOLD EDITION.

In Crown 4to vols. Now Publishing. Sixpenny Monthly Parts.

19 VOLUMES COMPLETED.

OLIVER TWIST, With 28 Illustrations, cloth, 2s. 6d. ; paper, 1s. 9d.
MARTIN CHUZZLEWIT, with 59 Illustrations, cloth, 4s. ; paper, 3s.
DAVID COPPERFIELD, with 60 Illustrations and a Portrait, cloth, 4s. ; paper, 3s.
BLEAK HOUSE, with 61 Illustrations, cloth, 4s. ; paper, 3s.
LITTLE DORRIT, with 58 Illustrations, cloth, 4s. ; paper, 3s.
PICKWICK PAPERS, with 56 Illustrations, cloth, 4s. ; paper, 3s.
BARNABY RUDGE, with 46 Illustrations, cloth, 4s. ; paper 3s.
A TALE OF TWO CITIES, with 25 Illustrations, cloth, 2s. 6d. ; paper, 1s. 9d.
OUR MUTUAL FRIEND, with 58 Illustrations, cloth, 4s. ; paper, 3s.
NICHOLAS NICKLEBY, with 59 Illustrations, cloth, 4s. ; paper, 3s.
GREAT EXPECTATIONS, with 26 Illustrations, cloth, 2s. 6d. ; paper, 1s. 9d.
OLD CURIOSITY SHOP, with 39 Illustrations, cloth, 4s. ; paper, 3s.
SKETCHES BY "BOZ," with 36 Illustrations, cloth, 2s. 6d. ; paper, 1s. 9d.
HARD TIMES, with 20 Illustrations, cloth, 2s. ; paper, 1s. 6d.
DOMBEY AND SON, with 61 Illustrations, cloth, 4s. ; paper, 3s.
UNCOMMERCIAL TRAVELLER, with 26 Illustrations, cloth, 2s. 6d. ; paper, 1s. 9d.
CHRISTMAS BOOKS, with 23 Illustrations, cloth, 2s. 6d. ; sewed, 1s. 9d.
THE HISTORY OF ENGLAND, with 15 Illustrations, cloth, 2s. 6d. ; paper, 1s. 9d.
AMERICAN NOTES and PICTURES FROM ITALY, with 18 Illustrations, cloth, 2s. 6d. ; paper, 1s. 9d.
EDWIN DROOD ; and REPRINTED PIECES, with Illustrations, cloth, 4s. ; paper, 3s.

Besides the above will be included—
THE CHRISTMAS STORIES.
THE LIFE OF DICKENS. By JOHN FORSTER.

Messrs. CHAPMAN & HALL trust that by this Edition they will be enabled to place the Works of the most popular British Author of the present day in the hands of all English readers.

MR. DICKENS'S READINGS.

Fcap. 8vo, sewed.

CHRISTMAS CAROL IN PROSE. 1s.
CRICKET ON THE EARTH. 1s.
CHIMES : A GOBLIN STORY. 1s.

STORY of LITTLE DOMBEY. 1s.
POOR TRAVELLER, BOOTS AT THE HOLLY-TREE INN, MRS. GAMP, 1s.

A CHRISTMAS CAROL, with the Original Coloured
Plates ; being a Reprint of the Original Edition. Small 8vo, red cloth, gilt edges, 5s.

THE LIBRARY

OF

CONTEMPORARY SCIENCE.

Some degree of truth has been admitted in the charge not unfrequently brought against the English, that they are assiduous rather than solid readers. They give themselves too much to the lighter forms of literature. Technical Science is almost exclusively restricted to its professed votaries, and, but for some of the Quarterlies and Monthlies, very little solid matter would come within the reach of the general public.

But the circulation enjoyed by many of these very periodicals, and the increase of the scientific journals, may be taken for sufficient proof that a taste for more serious subjects of study is now growing. Indeed there is good reason to believe that if strictly scientific subjects are not more universally cultivated, it is mainly because they are not rendered more accessible to the people. Such themes are treated either too elaborately, or in too forbidding a style, or else brought out in too costly a form to be easily available to all classes.

With the view of remedying this manifold and increasing inconvenience, we are glad to be able to take advantage of a comprehensive project recently set on foot in France, emphatically the land of Popular Science. The well-known publishers MM. Reinwald and Co., have made satisfactory arrangements with some of the leading *savants* of that country to supply an exhaustive series of works on each and all of the sciences of the day, treated in a style at once lucid, popular, and strictly methodic.

The names of MM. P. Broca, Secretary of the Société d'Anthropologie; Ch. Martins, Montpellier University; C. Vogt, University of Geneva; G. de Mortillet, Museum of St. Germain; A. Guillemin, author of "Ciel" and "Phénomènes de la Physique;" A. Hovelacque, editor of the "Revue de Linguistique;" Dr. Dally, Dr. Letourneau, and many others, whose co-operation has already been secured, are a guarantee that their respective subjects will receive thorough treatment, and will in all cases be written up to the very latest discoveries, and kept in every respect fully abreast of the times.

We have, on our part, been fortunate in making such further arrangements with some of the best writers and recognised authorities here, as will enable us to present the series in a thoroughly English dress to the reading public of this country. In so doing we feel convinced that we are taking the best means of supplying a want that has long been deeply felt.

The volumes in actual course of execution, or contemplated, will embrace such subjects as :

SCIENCE OF LANGUAGE. [*Published.*
BIOLOGY.   ,,
ANTHROPOLOGY.   ,,
ÆSTHETICS.   ,,
PHILOSOPHY.   ,,
COMPARATIVE MYTHOLOGY.
ASTRONOMY.
PREHISTORIC ARCHÆOLOGY.
ETHNOGRAPHY.
GEOLOGY.
HYGIENE.
POLITICAL ECONOMY.

PHYSICAL AND COMMERCIAL GEOGRAPHY.
ARCHITECTURE.
CHEMISTRY.
EDUCATION.
GENERAL ANATOMY.
ZOOLOGY.
BOTANY.
METEOROLOGY.
HISTORY.
FINANCE.
MECHANICS.
STATISTICS, etc. etc.

All the volumes, while complete and so far independent in themselves, will be of uniform appearance, slightly varying, according to the nature of the subject, in bulk and in price.

When finished they will form a Complete Collection of Standard Works of reference on all the physical and mental sciences, thus fully justifying the general title chosen for the series—" LIBRARY OF CONTEMPORARY SCIENCE."

LEVER'S (CHARLES) WORKS.

CHEAP EDITION.

Fancy Boards, 2s. 6d. each.

CHARLES O'MALLEY.
TOM BURKE.
THE KNIGHT OF GWYNNE.
MARTINS OF CROMARTIN.

THE DALTONS.
ROLAND CASHEL.
DAVENPORT DUNN.
DODD FAMILY.

Fancy Boards, 2s.

THE O'DONOGHUE.
FORTUNES OF GLENCORE.
HARRY LORREQUER.
ONE OF THEM.
A DAY'S RIDE.
JACK HINTON.
BARRINGTON.
TONY BUTLER.
MAURICE TIERNAY.
SIR BROOKE FOSBROOKE.
BRAMLEIGHS OF BISHOP'S FOLLY.

LORD KILGOBBIN.
LUTTRELL OF ARRAN.
RENT IN THE CLOUD and ST. PATRICK'S EVE.
CON CREAN.
ARTHUR O'LEARY.
THAT BY OF NORCOTT'S.
CORNELUS O'DOWD.
SIR JAPER CAREW.
NUTS AND NUT-CRACKERS.

Also in sets, 27 vols., cloth, fr £4 4s.

TROLLOPE'S (ANTHONY) WORKS.

CHEAP EDITION.

Boards 2*s.* 6*d.*, *cloth*, 3*s.* 6*d.*

2*s.* 6*d. vols.*

THE PRIME MINISTER.
PHINEAS FINN.
ORLEY FARM.
CAN YOU FORGIVE HER?

PHINEAS REDUX.
HE KNEW HE WAS RIGHT.
EUSTACE DIAMONDS.

2*s. Vols*

VICAR OF BULLHAMPTON.
RALPH THE HEIR.
THE BERTRAMS.
KELLYS AND O'KELLYS.
McDERMOT OF BALLYCLORAN.
CASTLE RICHMOND.
BELTON ESTATE.
MISS MACKENSIE.

LADY ANNA.
HARRY HOTSPUR.
RACHAEL RAY.
TALES OF ALL COUNTRIES.
MARY GRESLEY.
LOTTA SCHMIDT.
LA VENDEE.
DOCTOR THORNE.

CHAPMAN & HALL'S

List of Books, Drawing Examples, Diagrams, Models, Instruments, etc.

INCLUDING

THOSE ISSUED UNDER THE AUTHORITY OF THE SCIENCE AND ART DEPARTMENT, SOUTH KENSINGTON, FOR THE USE OF SCHOOLS AND ART AND SCIENCE CLASSES.

BARTLEY (G. C. T.)
CATALOGUE OF MODERN Works on Science and Technology. Post 8vo, sewed, 1*s.*

BENSON (W.)
PRINCIPLES OF THE Science of Colour. Small 4to, cloth, 15*s.*

BENSON (*continued*)—

MANUAL OF THE SCIENCE of Colour. Coloured Frontispiece and Illustrations. 12mo, cloth, 2s. 6d.

BRADLEY (Thomas)—*of the Royal Military Academy, Woolwich.*

ELEMENTS OF GEOMETRIcal Drawing. In Two Parts, with 60 Plates. Oblong folio, halfbound, each part 16s.

> Selections (from the aboveof 20 Plates, for the use of the Royal Military Academy Woolwich. Oblong folio half-bound, 16s.

BURCHETT.

LINEAR PERSPECTIVE. With Illustrations. Post 8vo, cloth 7s.

PRACTICAL GEOMETRY. Post 8vo, cloth, 5s.

DEFINITIONS OF GEOMETRY. Third Edition. 24mo. sewed, 5d.

CARROLL (John)

FREEHAND DRAWING LESsons for the Black Board, 6s.

CUBLEY (W. H.)

A SYSTEM OF ELEMENTARY Drawing. With Illustrations and Examples. Imperial 4to sewed 8s.

DAVISON (Ellis A.)

DRAWING FOR ELEMENtary Schools. Post 8vo, cloth, 3s.

MODEL DRAWING. 12mo, cloth, 3s.

DAVISON (*continued*)—

THE AMATEUR HOUSE CARpenter: A Guide in Building, Making, and Repairing. With numerous Illustrations, drawn on Wood by the Author. Demy 8vo, 10s. 6d.

DELAMOTTE (P. H.)

PROGRESSIVE DRAWINGBook for Beginners. 12mo 3s. 6d.

DICKSEE (J. R.)

SCHOOL PERSPECTIVE 8vo, cloth, 5s.

DYCE.

DRAWING-BOOK OF THE Government School of Design: Elementary Outlines of Ornament. 50 Plates. Small folio, sewed, 5s.; mounted, 18s.

INTRODUCTION TO DITTO. Fcap. 8vo, 6d.

FOSTER (Vere).

DRAWING-BOOKS:
(a) Forty Numbers, at 1d. each.
(b) Fifty-two Numbers, at 3d. each. The set b includes the subjects in a.

HENSLOW (Professor).

ILLUSTRATIONS TO BE EMployed in the Practical Lessons on Botany. Prepared for South Kensington Museum. Post 8vo, sewed, 6d.

JACOBSTHAL (E.)

GRAMMATIK DER ORNAmente, in 7 Parts of 20 Plates each. Price, unmounted, £3 13s. 6d.; mounted on cardboard, £11 4s. The Parts can be had separately.

JEWITT.

HANDBOOK OF PRACTICAL Perspective. 18mo, cloth, 1s.

KENNEDY (John).

FIRST GRADE PRACTICAL Geometry. 12mo, 6d.

FREEHAND DRAWING BOOK. 16mo, cloth, 1s. 6d.

LINDLEY (John).

SYMMETRY OF VEGETA-TION : Principles to be observed in the delineation of Plants. 12mo, sewed, 1s.

MARSHALL.

HUMAN BODY. Texts and Plates reduced from the large Diagrams. 2 vols , cloth, £1 1s.

NEWTON (E. Tulley, F.G.S.)

THE TYPICAL PARTS IN THE Skeletons of a Cat, Duck, and Codfish, being a Catalogue with Comparative Descriptions arranged in a Tabular Form. Demy 8vo, 3s.

OLIVER (Professor).

ILLUSTRATIONS OF THE VEgetable Kingdom. 109 Plates. Oblong 8vo, cloth. Plain, 16s.; coloured, £1 6s.

PUCKETT (R. Campbell).

SCIOGRAPHY, OR RADIAL projection of Shadows. Crown 8vo, cloth, 6s.

REDGRAVE.

MANUAL AND CATECHISM on Colour. Fifth Edition. 24mo, sewed, 9d.

ROBSON (George).

ELEMENTARY BUILDING Construction. Oblong folio, sewed, 8s.

WALLIS (George).

DRAWING-BOOK. Oblong, sewed, 3s. 6d.; mounted, 8s.

WALLIS (*continued*)—

DIRECTIONS FOR INTROducing Elementary Drawing in Schools and among Workmen. Published at the request of the Society of Arts. Small 4to, cloth, 4s. 6d.

DRAWING FOR YOUNG Children. Containing 150 copies. 16mo, cloth, 3s. 6d.

EDUCATIONAL DIVISION OF South Kensington Museum : Classified Catalogue of. Ninth Edition. 8vo, 7s.

ELEMENTARY DRAWING Copy-books, for the use of Children from four years old and upwards, in Schools and Families. Compiled by a Student certificated by the Science and Art Department as an Art Teacher. Seven books in 4to, sewed :

Book I. Letters, 8d.
„ II. Ditto, 8d.
„ III. Geometrical and Ornamental Forms, 8d.
„ IV. Objects, 8d.
„ V. Leaves, 8d.
„ VI. Birds, Animals, etc. 8d.
„ VII. Leaves, Flowers, and Sprays, 8d.

* Or in Sets of Seven Books, 4s. 6d.

ENGINEER AND MACHINIST Drawing-Book,16 Parts,71 Plates. Folio, £1 12s.; mounted, £3 4s.

EXAMINATION PAPERS FOR Science Schools and Classes. Published Annually, 6d. (Postage, 2d.)

PRINCIPLES OF DECORAtive Art. Folio, sewed, 1s.

SCIENCE DIRECTORY. 12mo, sewed, 6d. (Postage, 3d.)

ART DIRECTORY. 12mo, sewed, 1s. (Postage, 3d.)

DIAGRAM OF THE COLOURS of the Spectrum, with Explanatory Letterpress, on roller, 10s. 6d.

COPIES FOR OUTLINE DRAWING:

DYCE'S ELEMENTARY OUTLINES OF ORNAMENT, 50 Selected Plates mounted back and front, 18s.: unmounted, sewed, 5s.
WEITBRICHT'S OUTLINES OF ORNAMENT, reproduced by Herman, 12 Plates, mounted back and front, 8s. 6d.; unmounted, 2s.
MORGHEN'S OUTLINES OF THE HUMAN FIGURE, reproduced by Herman, 20 Plates, mounted back and front, 15s.; unmounted, 3s. 4d.
ONE SET OF FOUR PLATES, Outlines of Tarsia, from Gruner, mounted, 3s. 6d.; unmounted, 7d.
ALBERTOLLI'S FOLIAGE, one set of Four Plates, mounted, 3s. 6d.; unmounted, 5d.
OUTLINE OF TRAJAN FRIEZE, mounted, 1s.
WALLIS'S DRAWING-BOOK, mounted, 3s.; unmounted, 3s. 6d.
OUTLINE DRAWINGS OF FLOWERS, Eight Sheets, mounted, 3s. 6d.; unmounted, 8d.

COPIES FOR SHADED DRAWING:

COURSE OF DESIGN. By CH. BARGUE (French), 20 Selected Sheets, 11 at 2s., and 9 at 3s. each. £2 9s.
RENAISSANCE ROSETTE, mounted, 9d.
SHADED ORNAMENT, mounted, 1s. 2d.
PART OF A PILASTER FROM THE ALTAR OF ST. BIAGIO AT PISA, mounted, 2s.; unmounted, 1s.
GOTHIC PATERA, mounted, 1s.
RENAISSANCE SCROLL, Tomb in S. M. Dei Frari, Venice, mounted, 1s. 4d.
MOULDING OF SCULPTURED FOLIAGE, mounted, 1s. 4d.
ARCHITECTURAL STUDIES. By J. B. TRIPON. 20 Plates, £2.
MECHANICAL STUDIES. By J. B. TRIPON. 15s. per dozen.
FOLIATED SCROLL FROM THE VATICAN, unmounted, 5d.; mounted, 1s. 3d.
TWELVE HEADS after Holbein, selected from his drawings in Her Majesty's Collection at Windsor. Reproduced in Autotype. Half-imperial, 36s.
LESSONS IN SEPIA, 9s. per dozen, or 1s. each.
SMALL SEPIA DRAWING COPIES, 9s. per dozen, or 1s. each.

COLOURED EXAMPLES:

A SMALL DIAGRAM OF COLOUR, mounted, 1s. 6d.; unmounted, 9d.
TWO PLATES OF ELEMENTARY DESIGN, unmounted, 1s.; mounted, 3s. 9d.
PETUNIA, mounted, 3s. 9d.; unmounted, 2s. 9d.
PELARGONIUM, mounted, 3s. 9d.; unmounted, 2s. 9d.
CAMELLIA, mounted, 3s. 9d.; unmounted, 2s. 9d.
NASTURTIUM, mounted, 3s. 9d.; unmounted, 2s. 9d.
OLEANDER, mounted, 3s. 9d.; unmounted, 2s. 9d.
TORRENIA ASIATICA, unmounted, 2s. 9d.
PYNE'S LANDSCAPES IN CHROMO-LITHOGRAPHY (6), each, mounted, 7s. 6d.; or the set, £2 5s.
COTMAN'S PENCIL LANDSCAPES (set of 9), mounted, 15s.
    „   SEPIA DRAWINGS (set of 5), mounted, £1.
ALLONGE'S LANDSCAPES IN CHARCOAL (6), at 4s. each, or the set, £1 4s.
4017. BOUQUET OF FLOWERS, LARGE ROSES, etc., 4s. 6d.

4018.	„	„	ROSES AND HEARTSEASE, 3s. 6d.
4020.	„	„	POPPIES, etc., 3s. 6d.
4039.	„	„	CHRYSANTHEMUMS, 4s. 6d.
4040.	„	„	LARGE CAMELLIAS, 4s. 6d.
4077.	„	„	LILAC AND GERANIUM, 3s. 6d.
4080.	„	„	CAMELLIA AND ROSE, 3s. 6d.
4082.	„	„	LARGE DAHLIAS, 4s. 6d.
4083.	„	„	ROSES AND LILIES, 4s. 6d.
4090.	„	„	ROSES AND SWEET PEAS, 3s. 6d.
4094.	„	„	LARGE ROSES AND HEARTSEASE, 4s.
4180.	„	„	LARGE BOUQUET OF LILAC, 6s. 6d.
4190.	„	„	DAHLIAS AND FUCHSIAS, 6s. 6d.

SOLID MODELS, etc. :

* Box of Models, £1 14s.
  A Stand, with a universal joint, to show the solid Models, etc., £1 18s.
* One wire quadrangle, with a circle and cross within it, and one straight wire. One
  solid cube. One skeleton wire cube. One sphere. One cone. One cylinder.
  One hexagonal prism, £2 2s.
  Skeleton cube in wood, 3s. 6d.
  18-inch skeleton cube in wood, 12s.
* Three objects of *form* in Pottery :
  Indian Jar,
  Celadon Jar, } 18s. 6d.
  Bottle,
* Five selected Vases in Majolica Ware, £2 11s.
* Three selected Vases in Earthenware, 18s.
  Imperial Deal Frames, glazed, without sunk rings, 10s. each.
* Davidson's Smaller Solid Models, in Box, £2, containing—

2 Square Slabs.	Octagon Prism.	Triangular Prism.
9 Oblong Blocks (steps.)	Cylinder.	Pyramid, Equilateral.
2 Cubes.	Cone.	Pyramid, Isosceles.
4 Square Blocks.	Jointed Cross.	Square Block.

* Davidson's Advanced Drawing Models (10 models), £9. The following is a brief
  description of the models :—An Obelisk—composed of 2 Octagonal Slabs 26
  and 20 inches across, and each 3 inches high ; 1 Cube, 12 inches edge ; 1 Mono-
  lith (forming the body of the obelisk), 3 feet high ; 1 Pyramid, 6 inches base ;
  the complete object is thus nearly 5 feet high. A Market Cross—composed of
  3 Slabs, 24, 18, and 12 inches across, and each 3 inches high ; 1 Upright, 3 feet
  high ; 2 Cross Arms, united by mortise and tenon joints ; complete height, 3
  feet 9 inches. A Step-Ladder, 23 inches high. A Kitchen Table, 14½ inches
  high. A Chair to correspond. A Four-legged Stool, with projecting top and
  cross rails, height 14 inches. A Tub, with handles and projecting hoops, and
  the divisions between the staves plainly marked. A strong Trestle 18 inches
  high. A Hollow Cylinder, 9 inches in diameter, and 12 inches long, divided
  lengthwise. A Hollow Sphere, 9 inches in diameter, divided into semi-spheres,
  one of which is again divided into quarters ; the semi-sphere, when placed on
  the cylinder, gives the form and principles of shading a Dome, whilst one of
  the quarters placed on half the cylinder forms a Niche.
* Davidson's Apparatus for Teaching Practical Geometry (22 models), £5.
* Binn's Models for illustrating the elementary principles of orthographic projection as applied to mechanical drawing, in box, £1 10s.
* Miller's Class Drawing Models :—These models are particularly adapted for
  teaching large classes ; the stand is very strong, and the universal joint will
  hold the Models in any position. *Wood Models :* Square Prism, 12 inches side,
  18 inches high ; Hexagonal Prism, 14 inches side, 18 inches high ; Cube, 14
  inches side ; Cylinder, 13 inches diameter, 16 inches high ; Hexagon Pyramid,
  14 inches diameter, 22½ inches side ; Square Pyramid, 14 inches side, 22½ inches
  side ; Cone, 13 inches diameter, 22½ inches side ; Skeleton Cube, 19 inches
  solid wood 1¾ inch square ; Intersecting Circles, 19 inches solid wood 2¼ by 1¼
  inches. *Wire Models :* Triangular Prism, 17 inches side, 22 inches high ;
  Square Prism, 14 inches side, 20 inches high ; Hexagonal Prism, 16 inches
  diameter, 21 inches high ; Cylinder, 14 inches diameter, 21 inches high ; Hexagon Pyramid, 18 inches diameter, 24 inches high ; Square Pyramid, 17 inches
  side, 24 inches high ; Cone, 17 inches side, 24 inches high ; Skeleton Cube, 19
  inches side ; Intersecting Circles, 19 inches side ; Plain Circle, 19 inches side ;
  Plain Square, 19 inches side. Table, 27 inches by 21½ inches. Stand. The Set
  complete, £14 13s.
  Vulcanite set square, 5s.
  Large compasses with chalk holder, 5s.
* Slip, two sets squares and T square, 5s.
* Parkes's case of instruments, containing 6-inch compasses with pen and pencil
  leg, 5s.
* Prize instrument case, with 6-inch compasses, pen and pencil leg, 2½ small
  compasses, pen and scale, 18s.
  6-inch compasses with shifting pen and point, 4s. 6d.
  Small compass in case.
      * Models, etc., entered as sets, cannot be supplied singly.

LARGE DIAGRAMS.

ASTRONOMICAL :

    TWELVE SHEETS. Prepared for the Committee of Council on Education by JOHN DREW, Ph. Dr., F.R.S.A. £2 8s.; on rollers and varnished, £4 4s.

BOTANICAL :

    NINE SHEETS. Illustrating a Practical Method of Teaching Botany. By Professor HENSLOW, F.L.S. £2.; on canvas and rollers, and varnished, £3 3s.

CLASS.	DIVISIONS.	SECTION.	DIAGRAM.
Dicotyledon	Angiospermous	Thalamifloral	1
		Calycifloral	2 & 3
		Corollifloral	4
		Incomplete	5
	Gymnospermous		6
Monocotyledons	Petaloid	Superior	7
		Inferior	8
	Glumaceous		9

    ILLUSTRATIONS OF THE PRINCIPAL NATURAL ORDERS OF THE VEGETABLE KINGDOM. By Professor OLIVER, F.R.S., F.L.S. 70 Imperial sheets, containing examples of dried Plants, representing the different Orders. £5 5s. the set.

    Catalogues and Index to Oliver's Diagrams, 1s.

BUILDING CONSTRUCTION :

    TEN SHEETS. By William J. Glenny, Professor of Drawing, King's College. In sets, £1 1s.

    LAXTON'S EXAMPLES OF BUILDING CONSTRUCTION IN TWO DIVISIONS, containing 32 Imperial Plates, 20s.

    BUSBRIDGE'S DRAWINGS OF BUILDING CONSTRUCTION. 11 Sheets. Mounted, 5s. 6d.; unmounted, 2s. 9d.

GEOLOGICAL :

    DIAGRAM OF BRITISH STRATA. By H. W. Bristow, F.R.S., F.G.S. A Sheet, 4s.; mounted on roller and varnished, 7s. 6d.

MECHANICAL :

    DIAGRAMS OF THE MECHANICAL POWERS, AND THEIR APPLICATIONS IN MACHINERY AND THE ARTS GENERALLY. By Dr. John Anderson.

        This Series consists of 8 Diagrams, highly coloured on stout paper, 3 feet 6 inches, by 2 feet 6 inches, price £1 per set; mounted on Rollers, £2.

    DIAGRAMS OF THE STEAM-ENGINE. By Professor Goodeve and Professor Shelley. Stout Paper, 40 inches by 27 inches, highly coloured.

        The price per set of 41 Diagrams (52½ Sheets), £6 6s.; varnished and mounted on rollers, £11 11s,

    EXAMPLES OF MACHINE DETAILS. A Series of 16 Coloured Diagrams. By Professor Unwin. £2 2s.; mounted on rollers and varnished, £3 14s.

    SELECTED EXAMPLES OF MACHINES, OF IRON AND WOOD (French). By Stanislas Pettit. 60 Sheets, £3 5s.; 13s. per dozen.

    BUSBRIDGE'S DRAWINGS OF MACHINE CONSTRUCTION (50). Mounted, 25s.; unmounted, 12s. 6d.

MECHANICAL (*continued*)—

LESSONS IN MECHANICAL DRAWING. By Stanislas Pettit. 1*s*. per dozen; also larger Sheets, being more advanced copies, 2*s*. per dozen.

LESSONS IN ARCHITECTURAL DRAWING. By Stanislas Pettit. 1*s*. per dozen; also larger Sheets, being more advanced copies, 2*s*. per dozen.

PHYSIOLOGICAL :

ELEVEN SHEETS. Illustrating Human Physiology, Life size and Coloured from Nature. Prepared under the direction of John Marshall, F.R.S., F.R.C.S., etc. Each Sheet, 12*s*. 6*d*. On canvas and rollers, varnished, £1 1*s*.

1. THE SKELETON AND LIGAMENTS.
2. THE MUSCLES, JOINTS, AND ANIMAL MECHANICS.
3. THE VISCERA IN POSITION. THE STRUCTURE OF THE LUNGS.
4. THE ORGANS OF CIRCULATION.
5. THE LYMPHATICS OR ABSORBENTS.
6. THE ORGANS OF DIGESTION.
7. THE BRAIN AND NERVES. THE ORGANS OF THE VOICE.
8. THE ORGANS OF THE SENSES, Plate 1.
9. THE ORGANS OF THE SENSES, Plate 2.
10. THE MICROSCOPIC STRUCTURE OF THE TEXTURES AND ORGANS, Plate 1.
11. THE MICROSCOPIC STRUCTURE OF THE TEXTURES AND ORGANS, Plate 2.

HUMAN BODY. LIFE SIZE. By John Marshall, F.R.S., F.R.C.S.

1. THE SKELETON, Front View.	5. THE SKELETON, Side View.
2. THE MUSCLES, Front View.	7. THE MUSCLES, Side View.
3. THE SKELETON, Back View.	7. THE FEMALE SKELETON, Front View.
4. THE MUSCLES, Back View.	

Each Sheet, 12*s*. 6*d*.; on canvas and rollers, varnished, £1 1*s*.
Explanatory Key, 1*s*.

ZOOLOGICAL :

TEN SHEETS. Illustrating the Classification of Animals. By Robert Patterson, £2; on canvas and rollers, varnished, £3 10*s*.

The same, reduced in size on Royal paper, in 9 Sheets, uncoloured, 12*s*.

THE FORTNIGHTLY REVIEW,

Edited by JOHN MORLEY,

THE FORTNIGHTLY REVIEW is published on the 1st of every month (the issue on the 15th being suspended), and a Volume is completed every Six Months.

The following are among the Contributors :—

Sir Rutherford Alcock.
Professor Bain.
Professor Beesly.
Dr. Bridges.
Hon. George C. Brodrick.
Sir George Campbell, M.P.
J. Chamberlain, M.P.
Professor Clifford, F.R.S.
Professor Sidney Colvin.
Montague Cookson, Q.C.
L. H. Courtney, M.P.
G. H. Darwin.
F. W. Farrar.
Professor Fawcett, M.P.
Edward A. Freeman.
Mrs. Garret-Anderson.
M. E. Grant-Duff, M.P.
Thomas Hare.
F. Harrison.
Lord Houghton.
Professor Huxley.
Professor Jevons.
Emile de Laveleye.
T. E. Cliffe Leslie.
George Henry Lewes.
Right Hon. R. Lowe, M.P.

Sir John Lubbock, M.P.
Lord Lytton.
Sir H. S. Maine.
Dr. Maudsley.
Professor Max Müller.
Professor Henry Morley,
G. Osborne Morgan, Q.C., M.P.

F. W. Newman.
W. G. Palgrave.
Walter H. Pater.
Rt. Hon. Lyon Playfair, M.P.
Dante Gabriel Rossetti.
Herbert Spencer.
Hon. E. L. Stanley.
Sir J. Fitzjames Stephen, Q.C.
Leslie Stephen.
J. Hutchison Stirling.
A. C. Swinburne.
Dr. Von Sybel.
J. A. Symonds.
W. T. Thornton.
Hon. Lionel A. Tollemache.
Anthony Trollope.
Professor Tyndall.
The Editor.

etc. etc. etc.

THE FORTNIGHTLY REVIEW *is published at 2s. 6d.*

CHAPMAN & HALL, 193, PICCADILLY.

PRINTED BY TAYLOR AND CO.,
LITTLE QUEEN STREET, LINCOLN'S INN FIELDS.

www.ingramcontent.com/pod-product-compliance
Lightning Source LLC
Chambersburg PA
CBHW020938030726
47496CB00005B/1243